WHERE ONLY PRIDE REMAINS

Natalie Kleinman

SAPERE
BOOKS

WHERE ONLY PRIDE REMAINS

Published by Sapere Books.

20 Windermere Drive, Leeds, England, LS17 7UZ,
United Kingdom

saperebooks.com

ISBN: 978-1-80055-359-0

For Louis

CHAPTER ONE

While out riding with Captain Jack Staveley one morning, Prudence Fairham couldn't help but remark on the neglected condition of the estate. Jack had become a close friend ever since the day seven years ago that Angus — Prudence's father — had brought him to Fairham Manor when both were on leave. Jack being estranged from his own family, Angus had taken the raw young officer under his wing to such a degree that they were today like father and son, and Jack stood to Pru as the brother she'd never had. They had few secrets from each other, and his response reflected his sympathy.

"I am aware that the major has for many years during his absence left the handling of the estate to you and his steward, Simpkins. I also know that he is, forgive me, a better manager of men than of his inheritance."

They had slowed to a walk now and were able to talk comfortably as their horses were given free rein to stretch their necks. The hot spell they'd been enjoying for several days hadn't abated, and they agreed to halt and dismount by a stream which ran along one boundary so that Firefly and Storm could slake their thirst. They settled themselves on a fallen trunk which was thrown into shade by a weeping willow. Prudence laid her crop aside and removed her gloves, turning sparkling eyes to her companion, a sure sign of her pleasure in her favourite pastime, but her expression was otherwise serious. She wore a blue spencer jacket with braided piping which covered her riding habit of fine broadcloth. Topped as it was by a hat adorned with a blue feather, she was entirely unaware of how charming she looked despite the slight furrow between her brows. For her it was as much a part of who she was as the uniform worn by her father and his soldiers in battle.

"Simpkins and I have done our best, but I don't hesitate to confide in you, Jack, for you must know our circumstances almost as well as we do, that with my father's predilection for gaming, the funds available to us are irregular to say the least."

"It is the one thing in him that I cannot understand, for naturally we have played together many times. You, I know, looked upon our duties overseas as full of action. But between battles there were times, tedious times, when we had little to do but pull out a deck of cards to alleviate the boredom."

Pru looked at him quizzically, her head slightly to one side.

"It's true," he said, smiling at her. "Did you imagine we spent every hour engaging with the enemy? Your father loves to play but for some reason, and this is what I fail to comprehend, it is not for the game alone. The higher the stakes, the greater his enjoyment when he wins, and the deeper his despair when he is the loser."

"And it is not so with you?"

"Not in the least. I am as happy playing for straws. I'm surprised you don't know that, for you and I have played together many times over the years."

Prudence wound one of her golden curls between finger and thumb and pulled at it before it sprung back into place. It was an unconscious gesture that she employed often when she was troubled or deeply engaged in conversation. "I had thought, because I was merely a girl, that you…"

Jack laughed loudly enough for Firefly to lift her head and look at him with curiosity. "No such thing, my dear," he retorted. "'Mere' is an adjective I would never dare apply to you, and your skill is such that I wouldn't attempt to hazard a large amount for fear of losing my shirt."

He could see that she was still looking troubled and assured her that wherever possible he would try to curb her father's tendency to play above his means. Prudence knew he meant well but realised that this was an impossible task. They moved on to talk of other things but, as they rode back to the manor, Pru again looked around her at the land that was begging to be looked after, and her worry returned.

It was with no small degree of contentment that Pru leaned back in her chair and surveyed the scene before her. At the opposite end of the table sat her father, Major Angus Fairham, though she could see little of him, her view being obstructed by an ugly centrepiece which she had always disliked. She resolved once again to consign it to an unused attic room, heirloom or not. Ranged along either side were six gentlemen, soldiers every one. All but Jack Staveley had been previously unknown to her, but she was happy to have arranged this small gathering, for at long last her father was back from the wars. Whether or not he would be content to remain was a question she preferred not to think about for the time being. Angus was an adventurer, heart and soul, and little suited to a quiet life on his country estate.

Dinner over, Prudence dutifully left her guests to their port but it wasn't long before they pursued her into the drawing room, an altogether much more comfortable chamber with its couches and armchairs. The shutters were folded back and the windows left open to let in the evening air. A breeze tugged gently at the curtains and the fading light threw shadows onto a patterned but sadly worn carpet which Pru had long since ceased to notice. As he entered, Captain Staveley said with exaggerated affability, "I hope you will delight us by singing and accompanying yourself on the piano, Miss Fairham. I shall be happy to turn the pages for you." But he was unable to school his features into an expression of politeness to match his words.

Prudence laughed back at him, "What an abominable man you are, Jack, when you know my voice to be mediocre and my playing more so. Let me instead get out the cards, for I am sure that is something that will give us all far more pleasure."

"Impossible to resist teasing, but I still remember when first we met. You were, what was it, seventeen years of age, and your poor governess was trying so hard to instruct you in a skill that little suited your talents."

"Too true. The dear woman was convinced that no young lady's education was complete without learning to sing and play. And how she despaired when I would run off to the stables to see Angus's batman, Bunting. She never could understand how much I adored the man who had taught me the skill I love, or that I was as pleased to see him return home as I was to see my father."

"Probably more," Angus interjected, looking up with a grin from where he was pouring drinks for everyone.

"No, Papa, how can you say so?" Pru replied, the smile still playing around her mouth.

"Easily. Bunting has looked after us so well all these years and has shown us both far more patience than we show each other."

"That is because we are too alike, I fear."

"Well, he was certainly more able than I to curb your wilder tendencies."

"Whereas, with respect, no-one has yet been able to curb your own. You were far more likely to drag me along with you to face obstacles totally beyond my capabilities."

Angus looked at his daughter with affection, remembering hard gallops across the countryside, shoulder to shoulder. She had never feared to attempt any fence her horse was willing to take and had suffered many a tumble, only to berate herself for her own ineptitude and jump immediately back into the saddle.

The rest of the evening passed swiftly and in relative quiet as two card tables were set up and the participants concentrated on their game. The stakes being low, Pru was able to relax. Her father may have been an inveterate gambler, but he was also a good host and would not encourage his men to play beyond their means, even though he might on occasion do so himself. As similar to him as she was, it was a trait that Prudence had not inherited and could not understand. She concluded it was because she was a woman.

The soldiers were released from their duties the following week, but accustomed to living a life of action, they took every opportunity to indulge in whatever entertainments Fairham had to offer. So numerous were the trout hooked from the stream that many were returned to the water. "To fight another day, just like us," Rupert Fitzroy had remarked.

"But it would seem our fighting days are over, Fitz. When we return to the regiment, there will be drills and duties but no enemy to face in combat," Oliver Hervey had replied. "I for one am thinking of selling out and travelling the globe to see what adventure I can find. Who's for joining me?"

"Not I," said another. "The army is my life and who knows, with a bit of luck some trouble will flare up again somewhere and our services will once more be needed. How would it be if we all sold out? Who would protect our fair land?"

He spoke with passion but Fitz was looking at Olly thoughtfully, as though considering this new opportunity that had been presented to him.

"Well, I'm doing nothing in a hurry," said Jack, "other than taking these trout back to the house before they turn bad in this heat."

Angus did what he could to keep the men entertained. A fencing competition was organised at which Pru was permitted to keep score. A swimming race across the lake served to dispel some excess energy and to work up the men's appetites. A wild boar, caught on the estate, was roasted on a spit and satisfied everyone's hunger.

"Now I have a new challenge for you," Angus told them all one day as they were eating breakfast. "I have mapped out a route which we will all follow, but I defy any one of you to reach the finish before my daughter and her Firefly."

This was provocation indeed, and with Bunting acting as starter they set off at a pretty pace, each determined to prove his superior horsemanship. Pru, never one to refuse a dare, declared later that she'd had the best time. She did indeed win the race but insisted that she'd had the advantage because her knowledge of the terrain was greater than theirs. Thus the honour of all was satisfied, and Angus could be content that everything he had put in place had helped the men in the difficult transition from a state of war to a quite different way of life. Most were career soldiers and thrived on the discipline, but without any conflict the nature of their service would be very different.

After dinner, talk was often focused on their time in the army. Some of it had been hellish, Prudence knew, but a bond had been forged between them that would be hard to break. Jack was to remain at Fairham Manor before returning to his regiment. He no longer had a permanent place of his own and while in the military had no real need to look to this aspect of his future. He knew he was welcome to stay at the manor for as long as he wished, but he was also aware that when the time came for him to sell out he would have to buy a new dwelling. The funds for such an enterprise would not be a problem. Jack was a very wealthy man. Having the will was another thing; for many years now, the army and Fairham Manor had been the places he called home. For the time being he wished to change neither.

With the weather holding, Angus took every opportunity to be out of doors, seeking sport in the home wood, taking up again with old friends and neighbours, some of whom he had not seen for many years, and, though it seemed he was little interested in his estate, visiting his tenants at his daughter's behest. While he was thus occupied Prudence could be easier about him, but there was little doubt in her mind that there was an underlying restlessness. Though she felt it to be too soon after his return to consider travelling again, she raised the subject in the hope that it might divert him.

"I have been wondering, Papa, whether I ought not to replenish my wardrobe. If we are to travel abroad as you promised we should, I would like to be suitably attired. You assured me I might go with you when next you leave home."

"Said that, did I? Well, I have a fancy to take you to Paris. And to Rome, if you like." He hesitated a moment before continuing in a much more subdued manner, "I daresay you've been wondering why I've been avoiding talking to Simpkins. The place is falling to pieces, I know, and I am fully conscious that much of the blame must be laid at my door. I used to love it, growing up at Fairham then bringing your mother here upon our marriage. I was so proud of it in those days." He looked around the library where they were sitting, it being the coolest room in the house, but it was evident his focus was not on the book-laden shelves. Pru thought she had never seen him appear so sad. "That all changed when your mother died. If it hadn't been for you, Prudence…" He turned back to face her and the eyes that stared into hers seemed empty. "If it hadn't been for you, I think I might have put a period to my own existence. Everywhere I looked I could see Sally. It's no wonder I was half out of my mind. As it was, I did my poor best for you, but I was never at ease anymore. In the end it was the army that saved me. But that's over with now." Angus seemed to pull himself together. "So yes, which is it to be, Paris or Rome?"

Pru was shocked, for her father had never previously shown this side of himself. As close as they were, she had never before had any indication that he was fundamentally unhappy, for the face he showed her and the world was one of a man full of jovial humour and game for any lark. Trying to drag him away from his pain, she responded in kind. "Which is it to be, Papa?" she teased. "Why, who is to say it cannot be both? You must tell me, if you please, which fashion I am to follow. Do the ladies in Paris dress differently from those in Rome?"

"Some of the ladies do," he said with an appreciative gleam in his eyes.

"For shame, Sire, that you should speak to your daughter so. Not those ladies!" she said, happy to have been able to divert him.

"And what might you know of such, miss?"

"Only what you yourself have told me, you wicked man." By now both were smiling broadly. But Pru would never forget the desolation she had seen in his eyes.

There was a gentle knock on the door and both were pleased for the interruption. Jack entered the room at their bidding, saying as he came in that he had a mind to take out his fishing rod and would they like to join him.

"An excellent suggestion," Pru replied. "Is that where the others are? Do go, the two of you, for I have some housewifely duties to attend to. Are you meaning to go to the lake or the river? I would join you later if I may, after I have salved my conscience and appeased Mrs Jenkins. It never ceases to amaze me how all-consuming the subject of linen seems to be to her."

With something to do Angus became a changed man, eager for sport of any kind, and Prudence blessed Jack's intervention and the fact that he was to remain at Fairham after the others had left.

CHAPTER TWO

One morning after her ride Pru found her father's batman in the stable grooming the major's favourite mare.

"I have seen so little of you since you returned with my father. It's good to have you home, Bunting."

"Well, I'm certainly happier here than prancing around in them foreign parts, Miss Prudence. Not but what I think the major will want to be off again somewhere soon. Restless, he be, but then he never was one to settle for a quiet life."

She smiled and remarked that a quiet life and Major Angus Fairham did not in her opinion go hand in hand. "But we have discussed it and he has promised, when he goes travelling again, to take me with him, now it is safe to venture abroad."

"I do remember as how, when you were a girl, you talked of roaming the world."

"And who but you do I have to blame for that, pointing out all those faraway places on the globe in Papa's library. I learned far more from you than my governess, for you made it all so exciting. You have served us in so many ways over the years, John, and I must tell you that I took no small comfort knowing you were at my father's side. It was hard waiting at home, barely able to imagine the danger you were all facing."

Bunting paused his brushing, rested his hand on the mare's flanks and looked at Pru with understanding in his eyes. "It's as natural as breathing, miss, me being with the major. I were born on this estate and even though our birth meant we weren't of the same class, we grew up as boys together. He never pulled rank on me and has more than once honoured me by calling me a friend. And then, when you came along, apart from being a female, I could see your father in you all over again."

Pru laid her hand on his arm. "I'm grateful you didn't say *only* a female, Bunting, but even more glad that I too can call you friend."

"That you can, miss. Now be off with you and let me get on with my work."

"And now I feel again like the child I was when you sent me from the stables to attend to my lessons."

"Well, somebody had to."

"True. I was never the best of students."

"You were always a good student. It were just that your talents were here in the stable or learning to ride or to tool a carriage. Minding your stitches or poring over your books never suited you near as well. You should have been a boy."

"Greater praise I could not ask for," Pru said and returned to the house, chuckling all the way.

As she walked into the hall, Jack appeared from her father's library so she invited him to join her in the drawing room before going to her bedchamber to put off her riding habit.

"I was surprised not to find you waiting for me in the stables this morning. It isn't like you to miss the opportunity for an early ride."

"That's true for sure, but Angus wanted to talk to me before the others return to barracks."

"I've asked Cook to prepare something special for their last evening. I suspect parting from my father might be painful for some of those involved."

"I think you're right. We've served together for a long time. The major's retirement from the army will no doubt affect them all. He commands such loyalty that his men will be more than sorry not to see him again."

"And you, Jack? How is it that you are not yet returning to the regiment?"

"I am fortunate to have been granted extended leave and will remain here for a while longer, if you will have me."

"You are always welcome at Fairham. You know that." Pru tugged at a curl before continuing. "I am glad you are here. I fear Papa is already restless, and while I am more than happy to join him on his next adventure I think he would be well advised to rusticate for a while."

"It's one of the reasons I'm prolonging my stay. While I remain he will perhaps still feel the connection and be consequently less unsettled." He laughed, adding, "It won't do me any harm either. Fairham has become like home to me, but it is time I searched for a place of my own."

"Is there no chance of a reconciliation with your family?"

Jack thought of his own sire and shook his head. The hurt of their last communication was as fresh today as it had been all those years ago, Jack's only crime being that he was the recipient of his grandfather's vast fortune. Mr Staveley had, in indignation, sent a letter to him at Oxford:

I cannot understand why your grandfather would choose to bequeath his money to you, with no provision at all for your mother, or indeed your elder brother…

Jack could have enlightened him but did not do so. He would never forget his benefactor's words to him when he had earlier received a visit from him at college. "Don't like the man," he'd said of Jack's father. "Never did. Thought if he married my daughter I'd open my purse strings to him. Pure greed. He's full of juice and shamming it if he says otherwise. Don't need anything from me. He's perfectly able to look after my girl and your brother. You've never asked me for a penny, so it'll be you who has my fortune when I die."

And so it had been. Jack had been still at Oxford when his grandfather had passed away. Estranged from his family, for his father had stated, "You'll get nothing more from me, you may be sure of that," the young man had purchased a commission and had never returned, not even when on furlough. Jack had long ago transferred his filial affections to the major.

Cook did not let Prudence down. The feast that was spread on the men's last evening would have challenged even the most dedicated trencherman, and none of them was that. When the covers were removed they went one last time to the drawing room, where Prudence spent some time in conversation with Fitz and Oliver Hervey while the rest played cards. The hour was late and Pru, excusing herself, left them to their game and retired to bed. Olly and Fitz joined the rest and, as the candles burned down the betting became uncharacteristically deeper, perhaps because it was their last evening. Finally, all but Jack and the major had left the table, but the other men remained in the room to watch them play. The wine had been flowing freely and both men threw caution to the wind, little aware of their companions or indeed anything but the cards themselves. A silence fell as Angus, with nothing else to hazard, declared he would stake Fairham on the outcome of the game. Fitz moved to his shoulder and tried to intervene but the major, ape-drunk by now, was in no mood to listen. The card was turned. Unbelieving, he stared into the face of the Queen of Spades. He rose from the table to avail himself of ink and paper, upon which he signed over the home that had been in his family for generations. Jack tried to protest but he would have none of it.

"You have won fair and square," Angus said, managing with a supreme effort not to slur his speech. "Fairham Manor is now yours." With that he turned and left the room.

Jack, in little better state, was at least able to think clearly enough to say to the rest, "Never fear. Tomorrow I shall challenge him to a return game and I will ensure his property is restored to him."

With that, the gathering broke up and everyone retired.

The next morning the men took their leave of Prudence and Jack, for Angus was nowhere to be seen.

"I'm so sorry our visit ended as it did," said Fitz, taking her hand and kissing her fingertips.

"What do you mean?"

"No matter. Jack will tell you. I must thank you greatly for your hospitality, Miss Fairham. You have eased us all through a very difficult time."

He would say no more and by the time they had all left and she looked to ask Jack what Fitz had meant, he was no longer in the yard. She assumed he had returned to the house and went to look for her father, puzzled that he had not been there to take his leave of their guests. It was thus she discovered his letter when she'd sought him in the library. Angus had left it on the mantel above the ornate fireplace and her eye was drawn to it immediately.

My dearest daughter, I have failed you again, this time I fear beyond redemption. By the time you read this I shall be gone. You will go along far better without me. Do not feel I have...

Here the writing became a scrawl, the ink smudged, and it took a moment for Pru to decipher what it said. *Ah, I see,* she thought, after turning the sheet this way and that to catch the light. *Deserted you. I thought it said deserved you. Certainly I did not deserve this, for did you not promise that in future we would do everything together? It wasn't for you to decide. How could you? How dared you!* She read on, impatient to know more.

You are a young lady now and I have come to realise it would be unseemly for me to drag you all over the Continent in my wake. When recently I returned to Fairham Manor, I cherished the hope you would be married before the year was out.

But we were having so much fun, my darling girl. I didn't make the effort I should have to put you in the way of eligible young men. After so many years apart, I was too content with you acting as hostess to my friends, to our friends, when I should have sent you to your aunt in Bath.

Prudence sank to the floor, the note clutched to her bosom. *You did not look, when you spoke of my mother, as if you were having fun, Papa. But if it was so, why have you left me? What was so bad that we could not have worked it out together?* She looked again at the letter, searching for an answer. She soon found one.

It was the cards, you see. The cards and the brandy. It was like a fever in me and I couldn't stop. In the end I pledged the only thing I held dear, apart from you, Pru. Fairham Manor was lost to me on the turn of a card. The Queen of Spades, would you believe. There is nothing else. No funds, no other property. You will be secure, for you have your mother's legacy. No doubt, had I been able to touch it, I would have lost that too. Take it and go to your aunt. Live the life you were meant to. Know that I loved you. Papa.

A sudden commotion in the hall caused her to jump to her feet again and the door was thrust open unceremoniously.

"Miss Prudence, there's been a terrible accident," Bunting cried out in anguish. "It's the master. His horse came home without him and we found him in the home wood." He paused but there was no easy way to impart the news. "His firearm had exploded. We were unable to revive him." Tears ran unashamedly down his cheeks.

"What! Where is he? Take me to him," Prudence said, moving towards him with a stricken look.

"There is nothing you can do, miss. It's best you don't go."

The realisation dawned that her father had not, as she had first thought, run off to France without her. Prudence had lived since infancy without a mother and had long ago concluded that what one had never had one could not miss, but even with his chequered career her father had always been there for her. Not for a single moment had it occurred to her that one day her remaining parent would put a period to his existence in such a way and leave her alone in the world. But there was no doubting the grief in Bunting's eyes or the evidence she clutched in her hand. Angus Fairham had truly and irrevocably deserted her. With legs that refused any longer to support her, she once more fell to the floor. It was from there that Jack Staveley lifted her when he came into the room, hard upon the heels of Bunting.

When Pru opened her eyes, she was lying on a chaise longue in the drawing room to which Jack had carried her. As he turned to pour a reviving drink for her, she crumpled the paper in her hand and thrust it into the bosom of her dress. The restorative did much to bring her to her senses but with full consciousness came the gamut of emotions from rage, to despair and, finally, acceptance. It was instinct that had caused her to hide her father's letter, and now she resolved to show it to no-one. She was determined the world would believe he was the victim of a ghastly accident. Only his daughter knew he had taken his own life, though she conjectured that Bunting had his suspicions. He would have known there was little likelihood of such a careless mishap befalling his master as had been described.

Jack too was weeping, but angrily he wiped away the tears and regained control of himself. He was a soldier, after all. But what he told her next added sweeping rage to Prudence's already fraught emotions. "The world has turned upside down, but at least I can restore Fairham to you, Prudence."

"What are you talking about, Jack?"

"Last night, after you had retired, Angus and I sat down to play cards. That's what Fitz was talking about. We were in our cups, both of us. Well, all of us actually. You know how it is. To my shame you have seen us often enough in such a state."

"What has that to say to anything?"

"We've talked about the major's gambling, you and I. Last night it once more got out of hand. Terribly out of hand. But it was just a game to me. I resolved to reverse the situation when next we played."

"What are you saying, Jack?" But she knew already, of course. It had been stated clearly enough in her father's letter. Jack removed a paper from his pocket. This too was in her father's hand but it was quite different from the one she had secreted. It was his promissory note, handing over Fairham Manor and its estate to one Captain Jack Staveley. Prudence glanced at it and then up at him. "You should have stopped him! You of all people knew how it was with him!"

Jack took the criticism without demur. "To my shame I fear I was in little better frame than he," he admitted, and tried to press the note upon her. "Take it, or allow me to burn it on the fire."

She would not accept it. It was a matter of honour. He tried to argue with her.

"You must take it. Had your father not been the victim of a terrible accident, I would have ensured that we play again. That his home, and yours, would have been returned to him."

Only pride stopped her from breaking down. Pride and anger towards her closest friend. It seemed that Jack didn't suspect her father's suicide. To him perhaps it was inconceivable that the man he had fought alongside for so many years would take this way out. Easier to accept that fate had intervened with such a crushing blow before giving Angus the chance to win back his note. She would not burden Jack with the knowledge, she could not be so cruel, but neither could she forget he had been unwittingly instrumental in her father's death. This man who she had looked up to as a brother, the man she had considered near perfect, had flaws after all. She knew his grief must nearly match her own. Indeed, it had been Jack upon whom she had often relied for information when her father was abroad, Angus himself being a very poor correspondent.

"I ask again, Pru, that you remain at Fairham Manor. I will destroy this note. The rest will not breathe a word of what happened last night, and no-one else need ever know."

"You know I cannot do that, Jack," she said quietly but with steel in her voice, "for *I* would know. My father would not expect it of me, and neither must you."

"This is just foolish pride!" he shouted, pacing up and down, his anger at himself venting itself upon her.

"Maybe so, but I could not bear to be so beholden to you."

"You are being foolish beyond anything."

"Tell me, Jack," she asked, "were the circumstances reversed, what would you do?"

He had no answer, for she knew him too well. Jack reined in his temper. "What then will you do?" he asked.

"I shall go to my aunt. But in the meantime, I have a funeral to organise," Prudence replied, sounding as though she were in control but with her heart quietly breaking.

Prudence could never afterwards remember without pain that time between her father's death and her removal to Lady Channing's Bath home, where she was to remain for the foreseeable future. Her parting with her father's batman, Bunting, who had given her the confidence to back her first pony, taught her to ride with skill and courage, and to remember always to respect the animal that carried her. Saying goodbye to Mrs Jenkins, the housekeeper, who was to remain at Fairham Manor at the earnest request of Jack Staveley, and her husband, George Jenkins, who maintained the extensive grounds and had imparted to a younger Prudence a small part of his skill in the kitchen garden. All were to stay behind except her abigail, Kitty, daughter of the housekeeper and the gardener, who had clung to her parents and all those who were left behind in a way that Prudence longed to. It wouldn't do. She had needed to maintain her composure, or she would have broken down.

Jack handed her into the carriage. They had barely spoken since the day of the tragedy. Her anger had not abated. He had offered his escort to Bath but she had refused. The time had come for her to leave her home and she could not bear to prolong it. But as the carriage bore her away, she clung very tightly to the hand of the weeping girl beside her.

Prudence was no stranger to her aunt, having spent much time in Bath during her formative years while her father had been fighting for his country. Lady Channing had been instrumental in her come-out some years before. It had not served. None of the young gentlemen presented to Miss Fairham had sparked in her the slightest desire to spend her life with them. To the despair of her aunt she had refused three very flattering offers for her hand. Augusta had been desolate, conscious, in her own mind at least, that she had failed both her niece and her brother. In the intervening years Prudence had, when staying with her aunt, joined Lady Channing in her social engagements, but it was to no avail. At four and twenty years old she remained single, and her aunt had all but given up hope of a match for her.

Augusta had been surprised at the fortitude her niece had shown upon her arrival at Laura Place, for she knew the bond between father and daughter had been strong. It wasn't Pru's way, though, to wear her heart on her sleeve. Only Kitty had seen her distress, but in the end it was Prudence who had comforted the girl whose own tears had fallen unchecked.

CHAPTER THREE

Nearly six months later Prudence sat in her aunt's morning room, her hands resting in her lap. It was a comfortable room, the windows facing south to catch the sun. A dresser stood against one wall with Lady Channing's favourite figurines displayed thereon, and a likeness of one of her husband's ancestors hung above the fireplace.

Prudence's golden curls contrasted with the black of her mourning dress. The pallor of her throat and face was all the more evident against the dark crepe of her gown. Her chair, turned slightly towards the window, served only to allow the bright winter light from outside to accentuate the effect.

"Will you not take a glass of Madeira?" asked Augusta. "It will fortify you, perhaps."

Pru smiled at her but rejected the offer. "Thank you, but I need no such support. I fear it will muddle my already confused senses."

"Confused?"

"Only in as much as my period of mourning soon draws to a close and there is much to think about. With Emily's first season imminent you have enough to do. It can only add to your burden if you are determined to include me in your arrangements."

"Burden! You have never been a burden, my child," Augusta responded indignantly. She was distressed at the suggestion. Upon her brother's death, she had welcomed his only child with open arms as she had done so many times in preceding years.

"I am sorry. I didn't mean to offend you but only to acknowledge the extra exertion you have needed to make on my behalf."

Her aunt smiled, though it was more in the nature of a grin. She was a pretty woman whose vivacity showed in everything she did. "To be sure you have charming manners, and I am certain you did not learn those from your father."

"How can you say so, Aunt Gussie? Papa was perhaps the most charming man I have ever known."

The grin did not abate. "Oh, I grant you he was charming. It was his manners to which I referred. They were … somewhat erratic." Both laughed but Lady Channing, never one to lose her thread, continued. "However, I cannot agree with you on the subject of my exertions. Even in your grief you have been a delightful companion. I count it fortunate indeed that laying off of your black clothes comes at this time. You will soon need to re-enter Society. You will be company for each other, you and Emily, for I cannot hope when we venture forth that you will be engaged at every moment in conversation or dancing. One must be realistic about these things, after all. You are pretty girls and I have no doubt you will both be a success." Here she emphasised the word both, even though previous experience ought to have led her to view Prudence as a lost cause. "You will appear much more attractive to onlookers if you are seen to be in conversation with each other. Sitting demurely with one's hands folded may be engaging in its own way, but a more animated impression is given when talking with another."

"I see you have it all mapped out," Prudence said fondly, recognising the less than subtle objective behind her aunt's plans.

"One must be practical," Augusta said. "You are fair. Your cousin is dark. Already I have seen what an attractive picture you present when seated together. We must make the most of our assets, must we not?" she beamed.

Prudence laughed. In Aunt Gussie, though twenty years of marriage to Edward and the blessing of three daughters had perhaps given her an air of respectability, Pru had often observed a humour much like that of her father, though she perhaps lacked his intellect. Lady Channing's spouse too was a jovial man and his was a happy household.

The door opened to admit Miss Emily Channing, Prudence's cousin and at seventeen the eldest of Augusta's three girls, the other two not yet being out of the schoolroom.

"Papa has returned home, Mama. He is in his library and with him is Charles Wrotham."

Though she tried hard not to let it show, there was a hint of excitement in her voice. Emily, about to embark on her first season, had however fallen head over ears in love with the son of her father's greatest friend. It had seemed the attraction was mutual and it was hoped that the attachment would endure, for it would give great pleasure to both families. It wasn't talked of openly but Augusta had confided in her niece when they were alone. However, she was determined her daughter would enjoy some of her come-out before committing herself to matrimony, and indeed the young man had not yet declared himself, though it was judged to be just a matter of time.

Prudence, on account of her mourning, had not been included in the major part of her aunt's social life outside the home these past months. She had, however, met Mr Wrotham, no stranger to Laura Place, on several occasions, having been present when visitors came to the house. She liked him immensely and was delighted to see her cousin so happy.

Emily had been a source of immeasurable comfort during her time in Bath and she displayed a maturity not often seen in one so young. Prudence was able to talk unguardedly of her father without bringing censure down upon a much-loved but somewhat careless parent whose actions might have drawn reproof from another quarter. But the more Prudence spoke of him, the more she yearned for the freedom she had once enjoyed. There had been times during her parent's absences when she had not visited her aunt, but had remained at Fairham Manor, with only her old nurse, Peg, to serve propriety. Fond though she was of Lady Channing, she had enjoyed her independence. But Peg had retired two years since and gone to live with her family.

None in the Channing household knew how chafed Prudence felt and she would not for the world have caused her aunt unnecessary pain by telling her. In time that pain would be inevitable, for it was Pru's intention, once she was properly able to return to Society, to set up her own establishment, or even travel abroad as she and her father had planned. It seemed she might have to delay her objective, for she would not upset Augusta's wishes during the coming Season. She would be expected to help ease Emily's passage into Society and would do so willingly.

Edward Channing entered the room with Charles, and Prudence emerged from her reverie. "Upon my word, you are looking very fine today, Gussie," he said, bestowing an affectionate salute on his wife's cheek before turning to exchange greetings with the two younger ladies. Augusta blushed, but her husband was not a man to stand on ceremony. "We needn't mind Charles. He is almost one of the family," he added, sending his daughter, who sat now beside her cousin, into a state of confusion.

It passed unnoticed, as another visitor was ushered into the room and the footman announced, "Captain Jack Staveley."

Prudence, entirely unprepared, jumped to her feet and moved to clasp the captain's outstretched hand, her anger at him forgotten for the moment in her pleasure at seeing him again after so long. She saw the surprise in his face and recalled that they had not parted on the best of terms. Grief at the loss of her father, something she had over time been learning to live with, came once more rushing to the fore, and with it the memory of what had passed between them. She withdraw her hand and the light went out of her eyes, but she realised that her aunt's morning room was not the place to show her displeasure. In a polite but rather distant tone she said, "Jack, it has been an age. How are you?"

"I am well, thank you, and can only ask forgiveness that it has taken me so long to come and see you," he replied, hoping to recover some ground.

There was no warmth in Pru's voice as she replied, "Allow me to make known to you my uncle and aunt, Lord Channing and Lady Channing and their daughter, Miss Emily Channing. And Mr Charles Wrotham, a family friend."

Greetings were exchanged and, if her aunt thought Pru's welcome a little restrained, she was able to ascribe this to the opening of old wounds. Jack moved to stand by the fireplace, looking immaculate in breeches that served to accentuate the musculature of a fine pair of legs. His coat fitted closely over his broad shoulders and a cravat, simply tied, gave the impression of a man comfortable with but not overly fussed about his appearance.

"I say, sir, were you by any chance at Waterloo?" Mr Wrotham asked enthusiastically. "I was up at Oxford then, and by the time I might have purchased a commission it was all over." It was evident that Charles felt no little regret. In Emily's eyes he was a grown man, to be looked up to, but at only three and twenty years of age he still had all the eagerness of youth. His father's estate stood a little way outside Bath and it was there he spent much of his time, learning how to manage the place that would one day be his.

"Yes, I was fortunate to be so, and in the Peninsular before that."

"How I envy you. Did you know the great man?"

"From a distance only. I caught glimpses of him from time to time. You must know that I served with Miss Fairham's father. Indeed, had it not been for the major I would not be here today."

Prudence looked questioningly at him.

"You did not know, did you, that Angus saved my life when I was a very green soldier. We were in Salamanca and I would have been done for had it not been for him."

It came as news to Pru, though she was well aware that the captain had on at least one occasion pulled the major away from danger. It seemed that neither man had been in the habit of boasting of his own brave deeds, ready only to give credit to the other. It was something she had admired in her father and just another thing now to add to Jack's list of attributes. She sighed inwardly. It was a long list. Had it not been for his being instrumental in her father's death, she would still consider him to be her greatest friend in all the world. Was it time to stop blaming him for what had, after all, been her father's deed? She realised at last that she had spent these past months transferring her anger from the older man to the younger. Jack hadn't left her. Angus had.

"And where are you serving now?" Charles asked eagerly.

"I have only recently sold out. I've been stationed in the North these many months, which is why I was unable to pay this long overdue visit before now," he said, looking apologetically at Prudence.

She smiled and in a slightly warmer tone asked, "Do you remain long in Bath?"

"I have no immediate plans, other than to visit Fairham Manor. My only thought was to come and see you."

The words were spoken in a matter-of-fact way. Nothing in Staveley's voice indicated his trepidation. In truth he was a little apprehensive that Prudence might still blame him for the loss of her home. She could not, in his opinion, blame him more than he did himself. She received the statement in the spirit in which it was given, but Augusta was somewhat startled at this forthright manner of speech, though she could see nothing but friendship between the two. Surely, if Pru had a tendre for the captain, there would have been some indication of it in her manner. There was no such thing. A pity. His connection with Angus and knowledge of a life with which Prudence was so familiar would have made him an admirable suitor.

"If you have no permanent lodging, I should be honoured if you would stay with me, sir," Charles said. "My place lies just a short ride out of the city, and I would be happy to mount you during your stay."

"Thank you, my own horse is stabled at the inn along with that of my man. Your offer is very generous, Wrotham, but I do not wish to impose."

"There is no imposition, and I know I speak for my parents when I say they would be honoured to welcome one of our country's heroes to their home. Our stables are extensive and could easily accommodate two more horses. But of course I understand you may desire to make other arrangements." He certainly had no wish to embarrass the captain by putting him in a position where it was difficult for him to refuse his spontaneous invitation. But Jack laughed, a deep, warm sound.

"Not at all. You can have no idea how grateful I am. As a soldier I am used to being billeted in the most uncomfortable of circumstances. The inn where I have engaged to stay is well enough. Luxury even, after some of the situations I have been in. However, I should be delighted once more to spend some time in a family home. I thank you."

"Have you returned to Fairham Manor of late?" Prudence asked. She was aware that her aunt knew Jack was the new owner, though not the circumstances that made him so. Certainly Lady Channing was curious to know how the situation had come about, but etiquette demanded she did not ask and, though she had thrown out a hint on more than one occasion, no explanation had been offered.

"No, and my presence there too is long overdue. Bunting has visited two or three times to engage with your steward and reassure the servants they have not been forgotten."

"I am so glad Bunting went with you. I feared he would be lost without my father to take care of."

"He acted as batman to me as well as to the major. It is I who would have been lost. Would you care to join me when next I go to Fairham Manor, or would you consider it to be an ordeal?"

Lady Channing was shocked. It was not the practice for young ladies to gad about the country in the company of a gentleman, particularly one as handsome as the captain, and she was surprised he had made the suggestion.

Prudence laughed. "One glance at my aunt's face will tell you how she views your proposal. When do you go? I would like some time to consider your offer, if I may, but I am sure it would be acceptable, if Kitty were to come with me. No doubt she would be pleased to see her parents again. Do you not think so, Aunt Augusta?"

"We will discuss this later, if you please," Lady Channing said, firmly shutting down the conversation. She was concerned, for it was not in her power to dictate her niece's movements and she knew her to be unyielding once her mind was made up. Augusta did not fear that Emily might emulate her cousin. She was a dutiful girl, and Prudence's influence upon her had until now been a positive one. Her self-assurance and calm way of conducting herself served only as a good example to Miss Channing. What Augusta didn't know was whether or not her niece realised how damaging such an action might be to her own reputation.

"What's that? Are you off, then?" Edward Channing asked, interrupting his conversation with Mr Wrotham when he saw the captain move to take his leave.

"But you will come with me?" Charles asked.

"If you would be kind enough to give me your direction, I will join you tomorrow if I may. There are one or two things I must see to first, and I must settle my account at The Pelican."

Charles handed his card to Jack, and if Prudence felt regret at his leaving she did not allow it to show. If he was staying with Wrotham she knew she would see him again soon enough. How to persuade her aunt, without distressing her, that it was permissible for her to visit Fairham Manor in the captain's company was what was uppermost in her mind.

CHAPTER FOUR

"We have been invited to stay nearby at the home of a friend of Lord Channing. I believe it to be just a short ride out of town," Jack told Bunting when he returned to the inn. "We're to go there tomorrow."

"And Miss Prudence? Did you see her?"

"I did and she appeared in good spirits, though a little pale, I thought."

"Well, if she's been cooped up in town all these months I'm not surprised. She used to stride around the estate in all weathers with never a thought for her complexion. Not like some of the young ladies these days, with their bonnets and their parasols. Did you tell her of your plans to go to Fairham Manor?" Bunting asked, for he was entirely in the captain's confidence. Years of serving together, often in the most hazardous of situations, had rendered them more friends than master and servant.

"Yes, though I had unfortunately not taken the measure of her aunt when I did so. It will be hard, I think, to wrest her from the bosom of Lady Channing, who obviously disapproved of the friendly terms upon which we stand."

"Well, if I know Miss Prudence there'll be no stopping her if she wants to go."

Jack laughed, for there was no doubt that Pru would find a way of doing exactly as she pleased. But did she wish to return to her childhood home? He wasn't sure, even though she had professed herself willing. She had been pleased to see him, of that he was fairly certain, but would she, upon reflection, deem it a good idea to return to Fairham Manor with the very man who had taken it away from her? He looked again at Bunting, who was helping him out of his boots.

"I'm not entirely sure she wants to go back. It's been several months since she was there, and her last experiences were painful to say the very least. To lose the major in such a tragic accident and then her home as well... She may feel she doesn't want to be reminded of that time."

Bunting bit his lip. He had been on the point of letting the cat out of the bag and recalled just in time that the captain was unaware of what he suspected were the exact circumstances of Angus Fairham's death. So close had the two been that Jack, if he even suspected suicide, would suffer as much grief as Miss Prudence had done, for Bunting was in no doubt that she too had had her suspicions. He knew about the game of cards because Jack had told him.

"If only I'd had the opportunity to challenge Angus to another game," he'd said, running his hand roughly through his hair, as dark as Pru's was fair. "Worse yet was that I told Prudence of the circumstances. Had I only kept my own counsel she need never have known, but Fitz had already indicated to her that something was wrong and she demanded I tell her what it was."

Given time to consider, perhaps he might have fabricated some other reason for Fitz's comment, but his own grief had matched hers and the words were out before he'd realised the consequences. Never a day went by when he didn't remonstrate with himself. Unsure as to what his reception might be, Jack had thus far kept away from Pru and it had been with considerable trepidation that he'd visited Laura Place earlier in the day. Her greeting, after her initial surprise, had certainly been cool but it seemed after a few moments she had warmed to him again. He could only hope that their friendship might return to its previous footing.

"I'm not at all sure that Lady Channing was pleased at young Wrotham's invitation," he told Bunting. "I would not wish to go where I am unwelcome, nor do I desire to incur that lady's displeasure, but I will see Pru, if she wishes it, and staying with a family friend who is so obviously a regular visitor must make that easier."

"Well, Miss Prudence will make up her own mind, I'm sure. Would you like me to put anything out for you to wear this evening?"

"Thank you, but no, I have some business to deal with and will dine here. Check the horses if you will, Bunting, then do take yourself off if you wish. I shan't need you again until I retire. We will leave after breakfast. Here is the card. Perhaps you could find the direction and plan our route."

Jack sat at the small desk in his room and tried to concentrate on the papers he had brought with him. There would be much to do when he went back to Fairham Manor, but the timing of his journey there would depend upon whether or not Prudence was to join him. Estranged from his own family, he missed Angus more than he could say. Prudence was his connection to this father figure, but he had for many years called her a friend on her own account. Selling out, an action he had concluded to be preferable to remaining under the current circumstances, had necessitated leaving his army friends behind. A man of action, he had realised since that he needed a purpose in life if he was to find happiness. That purpose, he had decided, would be to restore Fairham to its former glory and in that way pay homage to the major. But would it be enough? He took a pen in his hand but stared unseeingly at the paper in front of him.

Pru had been planning her future for months. Not in detail, for the time wasn't yet right for that, but in principle she was determined to leave the shelter of Laura Place. While she could admire all that Bath had to offer, it seemed to her to be a place filled largely with acquaintances of her aunt and uncle, all very well in its way but lacking in stimulation for one with a lively mind and an even livelier sense of humour. The Pump Room, though a fashionable enough place to meet, was visited by many who took the water there in an attempt, misguided in Prudence's opinion, to ease their aches and pains. "Why do you persist in partaking of what is obviously highly distasteful?" she had enquired of Lady Channing when first taken there on a previous visit, laughing at the pained expression on that lady's face as she'd dutifully sipped while at the same time wrinkling her nose.

"But it is so beneficial, my dear niece. You must know that I always feel better after I've been here."

This was true, but Prudence quite rightly attributed the fact to her aunt's engaging with so many friends, rather than the medicinal properties of the water. Visitors to the Pump Room were not confined to her aunt's circle, but her present circumstances made it difficult for Pru to engage as she would have wished with those of her own age and interests. Naturally she could not attend the Assembly Rooms until she put off her black. Consequently, her overall impression was that Bath was fine enough but not the place where she would choose to reside indefinitely.

Pru was seated in her aunt's morning room with Emily when visitors were announced. They were poring over some dress designs at the time and presented just such a picture as Lady Channing had previously described, fair curls and dark mingling together as they leaned closer, the better to examine the details.

"Captain Staveley and Mr Wrotham," the footman announced. Both ladies looked up, startled, as neither had heard the discreet tap on the door, so engrossed were they in their task. Emily was aware her cheeks were flushed. Pru, happy to see Jack again and hoping they might return to their previous ease now she had put her anger aside, rose to greet the visitors.

"I had not looked for you again so soon," she said, addressing Jack.

"Wrotham here had an errand to perform for his father and insisted that we were so close it would have been rude not to enquire after the ladies," he replied. "It's a fine spring day. Perhaps, if you care to, we might walk to Sydney Gardens."

Emily, having barely recovered her composure, was once again thrown into confusion. "I'm afraid Mama is not home at present."

"There can be no objection if Kitty accompanies us, I am sure," Prudence said with a resolution her cousin found hard to resist, nor indeed did she wish to. Her misgivings cast aside, it required only that the gentlemen wait while each young lady fetched a bonnet and pelisse as there was a light chill in the air.

The four stepped into the sunshine with Kitty following at a respectable distance. Prudence, on Jack's arm, allowed the younger couple to draw slightly ahead, while still keeping sight of her cousin. Though Emily and Charles had known each other their whole lives, they were not now, when they most desired it, permitted to be private together. Pru had a soft heart and thought it could do no harm to give the pair some space. Her own easy exchanges with the captain were born of a greater maturity and the fact that she had spent a large part of her life in the company of the opposite sex. Her fingers did not tremble on Jack's arm, nor did she become tongue-tied when effectively alone with him.

She was surprised when he remarked, "They are well-suited, I believe. Will they make a match of it, do you think?"

"I hope so. Nothing has yet been said, but I believe there is an assumption that Mr Wrotham is holding back only because Miss Channing has yet to come out. If that is the case he is considerate indeed, but I feel certain he will attempt to fix his interest with her as soon as may be."

"And what of you, Pru? Do you plan to remain in Bath indefinitely?"

She turned her head and smiled up at him. "How well you know me. No, I plan to set up an establishment of my own. I know not where or how for the moment, but I miss the country and the freedom it gives me."

He stopped abruptly and, as if of its own volition, his free hand grasped hers where it rested lightly on his arm. "You must not, Pru," he said with some force. "Marry me and come with me to Fairham! I can give you back your home and the life to which you are suited. It was I, after all, who was instrumental in taking it away from you in the first place. You would be happier there, I'm sure, in the company of your old friends."

They stood motionless, unaware that Emily and Charles were drawing away from them and that Kitty was hard on their heels.

"How dare you!" The words exploded from Pru's lips, her face now flushed with an anger she had never experienced. "You would make me an offer out of pity? I had thought more of you, Jack. Did you really think I would accept? Does the sense of duty that made you fight for your country make you

41

also feel beholden to take my burden upon your shoulders? You should know me better."

The captain was as white as Prudence was flushed. His offer had come unbidden, a surprise as much to him as to her, and his motivation was a desire to afford her his protection. The pain of the past months had been hard to bear for a soldier who was wont to keep his feelings to himself. But he carried with him also the guilt of rendering the major's daughter homeless. Pru was right. He had proposed for all the wrong reasons and he felt shame at his outburst and sorrow at hers.

Kitty had drawn almost level with them and both became aware of their surroundings once more. Prudence was the first to speak.

"Say no more of this, if you please. How could you permit me to be so careless in my responsibility to my cousin? Come, they are almost out of sight. We must hurry and overtake them."

Jack took her elbow to guide her along the street but she shook him off, determined to show him she could stand on her own two feet, whatever the circumstance.

The next few days saw yet another shift in the relationship between Prudence and Jack. When he visited Laura Place, as he frequently did in the company of Charles Wrotham, none except Emily detected a difference in their exchanges, for both were at pains to behave as usual.

"Have you fallen out with Captain Staveley?" Emily had asked.

"Of course not. Whatever makes you think so?" Prudence answered, mortified that her change of attitude towards her old friend was evident.

"You seem less at ease when he calls, that is all. And today I saw you gripping the arm of your chair so hard that your knuckles were white. Forgive me if I am speaking out of turn, but you have been so good to me and I do not like to see you agitated. It is so very unlike you, after all."

"You could never intrude, Emily, but in this case you are mistaken. My discomfiture was on account of a sudden pain in my side which disappeared as soon as I stood. How kind of you to show such concern."

Prudence hated lying and had only done so as a matter of self-preservation. Thereafter she was more careful to maintain what had been her previous demeanour when the captain called. Jack himself was behaving as if nothing had happened between them, honouring her wish that it not be mentioned. He was doing it so well that she needed no further convincing that he had made his offer out of pity, and that was a thing she could not bear. Upon their return to the house in Laura Place and in the privacy of her own chamber she had shed many an angry tear, the worse for being pent up while they of necessity continued their walk to Sydney Gardens.

Once she had cried herself out, she splashed her face with water and sat down to take stock of her situation. Was Jack right? Would marrying him and living once more at Fairham Manor be preferable to the future she had mapped out for herself? No, Purgatory. To spend her life with someone who didn't love her was not to be borne. She would rather remain a spinster.

When Jack called again the following day, she was enough in control of herself that her outward composure fooled everyone but her cousin. She hoped she had reassured her, but it was a difficult path she was treading and it made her all the more determined to leave her aunt's home as soon as may be. For the time being, she wished the captain would take his leave and return to Fairham Manor. She had, as quickly as opportunity had presented itself, informed him that she would not be accompanying him. This she did while her aunt was present, knowing that once the statement was made it would be difficult to retract. She wouldn't change her mind and Jack made no attempt to persuade her. Two days later, he left Bath.

CHAPTER FIVE

Emily's launch upon Society proved to be very much as Lady Channing had predicted. The decision not to go to London had long ago been taken, the huge upheaval of removing the whole family to the capital being deemed unwelcome and Emily herself having no particular desire to be presented at Court. Both Prudence and Emily received much attention, Emily blossoming under her cousin's assured but amiable demeanour.

Aunt Augusta couldn't resist the temptation to repeat to her niece a remark made to her by an old acquaintance. "'What a pretty picture they make. A foil for each other, to be sure, and the contrast in their appearance an advantage to both.' That's what she said to me, Prudence. It's just as I told you it would be. It is to be hoped that all this attention doesn't go to Emily's head, but I pride myself on having raised her to be a modest girl."

"I am sure you need have no anxiety on that score, Aunt Gussie. My cousin is composed and without any of the meekness that seems to afflict so many young ladies when first they make their appearance on the social scene. Poor Mr Wrotham will be quite cut out."

"As to that, I don't believe so. You are aware that I accompanied Emily to her bedchamber when we returned from last night's soirée. She confided in me that, while she is flattered by the attention she is receiving and, to use her own words, enjoying being a grown-up, her heart is given to Charles. Bless the child, she was concerned at the expenditure her father is having to put out on her behalf, feeling it a fruitless exercise."

Emily had said as much to Prudence, so this intelligence came as no surprise. Pru had reassured her, explaining that her parent would want her to have every advantage and experience before settling down. She repeated this now her aunt.

"Yes, Prudence, that's just what I told her myself. 'A little town polish will do you no harm, my child,' is what I said. 'You will want to know, I am sure, how to conduct yourself when you are mistress of your own establishment.'" Here Lady Channing wiped away a tear for, even with two younger girls, she could hardly credit that her first born was old enough even to be thinking of leaving the nest.

"Do not distress yourself, Aunt Gussie. Consider instead that, if they do indeed make a match, Emily will be living only a very short distance away and, with the friendship between their fathers, I make no doubt you will see almost as much of her as you do now." This was, of course, an exaggeration, but it served for the moment to settle her aunt's jangled nerves.

Though Lady Channing had been correct in her assertion that two young ladies in animated conversation were more attractive than one sitting demurely but expectantly alone, there was little time for conversation when attending any function where dancing was taking place. Prudence and Emily were solicited for almost every dance and, when not whirling around the floor, they could be seen with a number of gentlemen paying court to them where they sat.

Prudence, released from her mourning, was delighted to participate in an activity she had always enjoyed. She was an accomplished and assured dancer. On those occasions when her father had been home and had entertained their neighbours or his fellow officers, she had become accustomed to standing up for country dances and even for the daring but now almost universally accepted waltz, and was not therefore put out of countenance when held in some gentleman's arms. She could not, however, dismiss from her memory the times she had performed that very dance with Captain Staveley. Nor could she help wondering if he remained at Fairham Manor or had moved on. It seemed more likely that he would have taken up residence there, for she knew he had no other permanent home in England. She could only speculate. Jack had not written to her since leaving Bath and, though it had been only three weeks since, she was disappointed not to have received news of her former home. But it seemed he had taken her dismissal of him to an extreme she had not anticipated. She began to wonder if she would ever hear from him again.

All three ladies were seated one day in Lady Channing's morning room when a visitor was announced. The name meant nothing to the two younger girls, but Augusta's reaction was writ plainly in the frown upon her face before she rose and composed her features into an expression of welcome.

"My word, Gussie, you have become quite plump since last I saw you," said the vivacious woman who entered with all the assurance of a lady of some forty summers.

"Rebecca, how delightful to see you after all these years," Lady Channing replied with more good manners than truth. "Allow me to make known to you my eldest daughter, Emily, and Prudence —" here she paused before continuing to no little effect — "your niece. Girls, this is Rebecca Standish. Your mother's sister, Prudence."

"But how can this be?" an incredulous Prudence asked, moving towards the newcomer. "I was never told my mother had a sister." Arms were opened and she walked into their embrace before stepping back in wonder to look at this new relation. "Why was I never told of this?"

Rebecca laughed, a delightful sound. "I fear I was the black sheep of the family. Resisting all attempts to marry me off to some lord or other, I forget his name, I ran away with Standish and was disowned forthwith."

Augusta interrupted only to beg that they all be seated and looked anxiously at her daughter, for there was no doubt that Rebecca had charm and to sully Emily's ears with talk of an elopement was not what her mother liked. Not at all.

"But this is infamous," Prudence said. "I can understand that when I was a child my father might have wished to keep this from me, but his own career was not so without blemish that he should sit in judgement upon another. Surely, when I was older, he ought to have told me."

Mrs Standish smiled hugely. "I expect he forgot all about it, though he might of course have mentioned meeting me once or twice in his letters home as I was forever running into him on the Continent. An enchanting companion. I'm not at all surprised Sally was so in love with him. A pity she died so young."

This last was said with no apparent regret on her own part for the loss of her sister, and Prudence bridled for a moment until she realised that if she ever spoke of her mother it was in that same matter-of-fact way. In any case, she was far too intent on finding out what she could to be waylaid by something that had happened so long ago.

"You knew my father!" she exclaimed.

"Very well. In the lull between engagements he was a welcome addition to the social calendar. A very pretty dancer, as I recall. He and that handsome young captain who would so often accompany him."

One more grievance to hold against Jack, Prudence thought, for her Aunt Rebecca could be referring to no other young captain.

Lady Channing could tell this visit might be of some duration and, bowing to the inevitable, she rang the bell for tea. An hour later Rebecca Standish rose and took her leave, but not before she had arranged to see her niece again on the following day. They were to meet in the Pump Room where Prudence would be escorted by a footman, her aunt being chaperone enough when she arrived. In the short time Rebecca had remained in Laura Place, Pru had learned three things. Lady Channing was apprehensive of her visitor, Rebecca was widowed and childless and, above all, Pru liked her immensely. When they met for the second time it was as if they had known each other all their lives.

"I was surprised, though perhaps I ought not to have been, at the resemblance between you and Sally. You are barely older now than my sister was when last I saw her, and it almost could have been her standing before me yesterday," Rebecca said.

"This is another thing that no-one has ever told me before," Prudence replied. "I am said to be like my father in my character and never gave a thought to whom I might favour. I cannot believe I was so kept in the dark, nor do I understand why, Aunt Rebecca."

"For heaven's sake call me Becky, for I hope I'm not in my dotage yet and Aunt Rebecca makes me feel so old," she said with her ready laugh.

"No-one could level that at you, for sure," Prudence said, her own smile lighting up her face. And it was true. Becky's figure was as trim as a girl's half her age and her complexion owed nothing to any artificial aids. "And you must call me Pru, for I believe my nature does not match my name," she added, aware that imprudence at times befitted her far better. "But tell me, for I could see you were under some constraint when talking with my aunt yesterday, what are your plans now you are back in England?"

"Well, with poor Standish dead these twelve months but fortunately leaving me in a position to indulge any whim, I thought it time to return. The truth is, Prudence, you are my only living relative and I wanted to meet you." She spoke flippantly but there was sadness in her eyes.

"And I am glad you did, for I might have gone on forever not knowing my mother had a sister and I an aunt of whom I am growing fonder with every passing moment," Pru said with a frankness and a ready smile that matched Rebecca's. "Tell me, if you please, and if it's not too painful, what happened to my uncle. He must have been a young man. Was it an illness that carried him off?"

Rebecca laughed loudly enough for those close by to look round at her but she wasn't put out by their disapproval, if disapproval it was. And it wasn't long before Prudence was laughing too. What Becky told her was shocking indeed, but the manner of her telling held so much humour that her niece enjoyed the tale, as it was intended she should, for despite her underlying grief she rejoiced in her husband's actions.

"Nothing so mundane, my dear. He was shot! Yes, I can see I've surprised you, but I was hardly myself surprised. Standish was defending my honour, as he had on many occasions over the years. He was a dashing man. It was that which drew me to him in the first instance. You will have observed that I am not of a self-effacing character." She paused, the smile in evidence again. "It has on occasion attracted attention from admirers that went beyond what my husband felt acceptable and he was forever challenging people to a duel, even in later years when duelling was no longer fashionable. While I enjoyed a light flirtation now and again there was never anything serious, as well he knew, but he was such a romantic figure and truly enjoyed what he considered to be protecting my virtue. Alas, his own weapon misfired and his opponent's bullet found its target. Standish was no more."

Prudence tried hard to look sympathetic, but it was evident that Becky had come to terms with her loss and was proud of her spouse. She learned that they had been devoted to each other and it had taken time for the widow to contemplate what her future was to be without him. Living aimlessly for some months, ultimately she had decided to return to England to seek out her niece. She had travelled first to Fairham Manor, unaware of the untimely death of her brother-in-law, only to find Captain Staveley the new incumbent. He it was who had given her Pru's direction and so she had travelled to Bath. "He asked that I tell you all is well at your former home and he would be happy to see you whenever you might choose to return." Pru wasn't sure what to make of this message. Was there some hidden meaning or was Jack merely being polite? As for Becky, what she was to do next very much depended upon whether her niece wished to pursue their relationship.

"Where are you staying, Becky?" Prudence asked, the name tripping easily off her tongue.

"At the Sydney Hotel. It will do for the time being until I can decide where my future lies. In the meantime, it is a joy to know that I have such a pretty and vivacious niece whom I sincerely hope loves shopping as much as I do, for there are many things I need to buy."

Pru's laugh was as infectious as her aunt's. "If you may tell me the woman who does not like shopping I should like to meet her. There are several excellent establishments in Bath, as

I have discovered. We should begin in Milsom Street, where I had the pleasure of spending much time recently when putting aside my mourning clothes. It is said to rival Bond Street in London, though I have never been there so I am not in a position to judge."

"Would you care to go to London?"

"Not especially. I am a country girl at heart and the hustle and bustle of Bath offers sufficient excitement for one of my particular likes."

The two chatted amiably. Far from finding it difficult to light upon topics that interested both, they found the time flew by and all too soon Prudence had to return to Laura Place where Aunt Gussie was entertaining and required her presence. Becky had not been invited, the gathering having been arranged prior to her arrival, but it was doubtful in any case that she would have received an invitation. While it was not her business to discourage an association between her niece and her other aunt, Pru was aware of Lady Channing's disapproval of the circumstances leading to Mrs Standish leaving the country, and that the passing years had not brought about any relaxation in that view.

"Milsom Street it is, then," Prudence exclaimed as they parted company. "Tomorrow, if you are free, and perhaps we may afterwards take refreshment at Sally Lunn's, for it is a superior place and well-deserving of its reputation."

Returning to Laura Place, Pru had little time to herself for the rest of the day, having room for reflection only when at last she entered her bedchamber for the night. There was no doubt in her mind that in Rebecca Standish she had found a friend and an idea, hazy at first, began to take shape. She would sleep on it.

But sleep didn't come easily. She wondered about Jack's message to her. Was he being merely polite? Did his conscience prey upon him? She couldn't know, of course. She knew only that she missed his friendship. Could they put that horrible proposal behind them and renew their old easy ways? She was still so exceedingly angry with him for, try though she might, she could not forget that in some measure he had been the cause of her father's death. She could not truly blame him. Angus Fairham had taken his own life, his was the finger that had pulled the trigger. But that trigger would not have been pulled had it not been for the careless action of two men in their cups. And had Jack not promised her he would try to curb her father's gambling tendencies, only to be present on that dreadful night?

His untimely offer had made Pru even angrier. She had left Jack in no doubt as to how she felt, not for one moment dreaming he would see it as a complete cutting of their friendship. Well, now he had offered her an olive branch of sorts, whether intentional or not. Tomorrow morning she would write to him to thank him for his invitation, which of course she would decline, and to enquire after the members of the household who had looked after her all her life. It was to be hoped this would once more open the line of communication between them, albeit it tenuous. With that thought in mind, finally sleep enfolded her in its welcoming arms.

Waking early, but hardly refreshed after a disturbed night, Pru sat at her dresser to compose a letter to Jack. Their correspondence was of many years standing but on this occasion the words, which normally would have flowed almost unthinkingly through her pen, refused to come. Her golden curls were unrestrained and fell gently about her face. Sparkling sapphire-blue eyes softened at the thought of the handsome soldier whom she had held in such affection these past few years. What a pity, now he had sold out, that she would never again see him in uniform. The ink had dried on the end of her quill and she dipped it once more into the well.

My dear friend,

I thank you for your kind invitation to Fairham Manor. You will understand, I am sure, the reasons why I feel unable to return at this time. Do not, I pray, distress yourself. I have accepted my situation and am busily engaged in making plans for my future. In the meantime, I would look upon it as a favour if you would convey my good wishes to all who looked to my comfort for so many years. I think of them often and would not wish them to believe I had forgotten their kindness to me. I beg you will ask George Jenkins to continue to care for the small patch of kitchen garden which he assigned to me long ago.

You will know, for you sent her to me, that I have now made the acquaintance of my mother's sister. I cannot believe I was never told of her existence. Was there some conspiracy of silence, for surely the circumstances are such that you and I would have laughed at them? Becky did when she gave me a full account of her youthful exploits. I feel sad that I never had the opportunity of meeting Standish, for he sounds to have been a very flamboyant man. She will find it difficult, no doubt, now that he is gone, but we have struck up such a close friendship in a short space of time, I feel certain that we will each be a support to the other going forward.

I know you will have much to occupy you at Fairham Manor. Simpkins and I did our best during my father's long absences but I fear the estate, if not the house itself, is sadly in need of attention. I hope you do not regret your 'windfall'.

My last message is for Bunting, who has looked after us all for so many years. Tell him, please, that I hope one day to ride with him again and

that I have never forgotten the time when he helped a very excited but
nervous child onto the back of her first pony.

 Yours with affection as ever,
 Pru

Prudence thought it wise not to mention their falling out. Safe in the knowledge that she was unlikely to see Jack in the foreseeable future she wanted, nonetheless, to ensure that the connection was not completely severed. Their often infrequent exchange of letters had been a straw to which she had clung for so long and was now the one aspect of her old life that remained to her. She was not yet ready to let it go. She re-read the letter. Not altogether satisfied but feeling it would have to do, for it left open the possibility of future correspondence, she rose from the chair to get on with her day.

She was excited at the prospect of shopping with Becky but more so of posing her idea to her recently widowed aunt. What would she make of Pru's suggestion?

CHAPTER SIX

It was a fine spring day and Pru was waiting impatiently in Laura Place for Becky to arrive. The latter had chosen to walk from the Sydney Hotel along Great Pulteney Street. Together they crossed the bridge and were soon delighting themselves among the treasures to be found in Milsom Street.

"I dare say this lace is as fine as any I ever saw in Brussels," Becky remarked, holding the fabric between her fingers. "And the embroidery on the sleeves of this evening dress is absolutely exquisite."

Pru delighted in her aunt's pleasure and, having so recently replenished her own wardrobe and mindful of her circumstances, she forbore purchasing another gown, though her reticule had seen better days and she was unable to resist a particularly charming poke bonnet which Becky said framed her face to perfection. Two very happy but tired ladies finally stopped for refreshment at Sally Lunn's, having arranged for their parcels and boxes to be transported either to Laura Place or to Becky's hotel.

"What a dowd you must think me, Pru. I had believed, erroneously as it turns out, that I was all the crack. I see now I was sadly mistaken. How fortunate that Standish left me in such a way as not to be purse pinched, for a return visit to Milsom Street is imperative. Even two returns," Becky said with her contagious laugh.

Her ease gave Prudence the courage to broach the subject that had been on her mind. Her whole future rested on her aunt's response.

"Forgive me if I am overstepping the mark but you did say, did you not, that you sought me out as your only living relative. Since we met I have formed the opinion that you are uncertain as to how you will move forward after my uncle's passing." She paused because, in spite of Becky showing a brave front, Pru had come to realise that beneath her frivolity there lay a thoughtful and caring woman who had but recently lost the man she had loved. A pained expression flashed across her aunt's features but she did not speak. Pru continued, "You will know that upon my father's death Fairham Manor fell not to me but to Captain Staveley. Aunt Augusta has been kind enough to furnish me with a home, but it has always been in my mind to set up my own establishment." If she had expected the usual recrimination from Becky it did not come, and the smile she almost habitually wore returned.

"Gussie will not approve of that, for sure."

"You are right, of course. She has said as much." Pru paused again, collecting her thoughts and trying to find the best way to express herself. Finally, and in her usual fashion, she came straight to the point. "She could not object, however, if I were to take up residence with my other aunt, could she?"

What occurred next left Prudence mortified, for she was astonished to see large tears form in Rebecca's eyes and tumble down her cheeks. Pru was all apology, grasping the other's hands and begging forgiveness for upsetting her. She had not meant to distress her, she said. She had thought only that it was a way forward for them both. She wouldn't say another word on the matter and she begged her aunt not to cry.

"It is to be hoped that you will say several more words on the matter, my dear, for nothing would please me more," Becky said, wiping away her tears. "You are right, of course, and I have been bending my mind trying to decide what to do.

I never dreamt of this as a solution, but it seems it would suit us both. How clever of you to think of it. But there is much to talk about. Where would you choose to live? Here, in Bath?"

For the first time in months Pru felt as though a huge weight had been lifted from her. There was a clear path before her and the only obstacle, Society's opinion of a single young woman living on her own, was removed entirely. Not that she cared much for Society's opinion, but Aunt Gussie did and it would have been unkind and unfeeling of her not to have worried on that account. Emily no longer had need of her support, for Charles had offered for her only the previous evening, and had been accepted. Nothing remained to hold her in Laura Place except her affection for her aunt and uncle and she hoped she would be welcomed whenever she chose to visit, but live with them forever she could not. Already the restrictions that were placed upon her were beginning to chafe.

"Not in Bath, no. I would choose to go home."

"To Fairham?" was the astonished reply.

"No, not to Fairham, of course, but to Somerset. To be close to the friends and neighbours I have not seen for so long. To ride familiar fields and lanes. To be free to entertain as I did before, even when my father was abroad, without incurring the disapproval of those around me. In short, to be once again my own mistress."

Pru had become more animated with every word. Her pulses were racing as at last she envisaged a life of her own choosing.

At Fairham Manor Jack had been finding it no less difficult than Pru in searching for a way forward. The army had been his life for all his adult years and Major Fairham had been a part of it for as long. Now both were gone, and his new home was a constant reminder of the past. Jack, never the one to kick his heels, was chafed beyond bearing by the enforced inactivity. It was time, he decided, to do something about it.

He was out riding one morning, unconsciously tracing the path Angus had taken on that fateful day nearly a year ago. A good canter had helped clear his mind and he brought his horse to a walk as they entered the home wood. It had been a favourite place in times gone by when, on furlough, he and the major had gone hunting for sport. Dismounting in a clearing he tethered Storm to a tree, his cream mane and tail, moments earlier flying in the wind, now resting against his golden coat. Patting his neck, Jack murmured softly in his ear before sitting down on the trunk of a fallen oak. It was here, he knew, that the accident had taken place, for Bunting had, at the captain's insistence, reluctantly led him months ago to the spot where the major's body had been found. There were many roots protruding from the ground and it was not inconceivable that Angus had tripped over one of these, causing his firearm to explode, cocked as it may have been for whatever game was to be found. Jack had accepted Bunting's account without question and today his thoughts were on the future, not dwelling on the past.

"Well, Major, it is time I made a decision, is it not?" he said aloud and the sound of his own voice out there in the open, with none but the birds and Storm to hear, echoed strangely in his ears. It was in a way comforting and aided him in formulating his ideas and clearing his head. "I have been idle far too long. I need some purpose to my life and, while I know you will forgive me for saying that Fairham is in need of attention, it will not be enough to occupy a man so accustomed to action as I have been. I have no wish to travel. I've done as much in my lifetime as a man could want. I believe I have found the answer."

He paused, thinking that at least there was communication again between him and Prudence. He could use her former home as a reason to maintain their correspondence, on the assumption that she would be interested, at the very least, in knowing what was happening with the place, and with her retainers. Following his reply to her letter, assuring her he would pass on her messages, they had resumed their correspondence and seemed as before, but Jack was no fool. He could, between the lines, read another line which he would cross at peril of again incurring her rage. He knew what a cawker he had made of himself. Of course she'd rejected his offer. Any woman would have done the same. He could only be glad that he'd given Rebecca Standish her direction, for it seemed the two had struck up a firm friendship. He was aware now that they planned to set up home together and could only be glad both had found some kind of solution to their respective difficult situations. Jack was flattered to still be the recipient of Pru's confidences. He only wished there was more. Fairham Manor was not the same without her. Sighing, he resumed his one-sided conversation with Angus.

"I have a plan, Major, and it's one of which I feel certain you will approve. There have been nights when I have had little sleep, when visions of the battlefield swim before my eyes, as clear in the dark as in those dreadful days when a relentless sun shone down on us in the heat of the fighting. And what I see is the horror of war. Trampled bodies, lying in the mud, never to return home to their families. Young men, laid out on makeshift litters, or even on the ground, in the field hospital. The moans and cries of pain. A shattered shoulder. A severed arm. One leg where once there were two. And then, well, this is where I come to the point. Last night I awoke with a start. I sat up in bed, covered in sweat, as is usually the case when I have these dreams. But as I sat there I smiled. For I have found my goal, Angus."

And he had. It was a more relaxed man who permitted his thoughts to wander, relieved at last to have an aim after being idle for so long. He would build a hospital for those whose wounds were still in need of attention, as well as a rehabilitation centre and, if necessary, a permanent home. They would be sited in the grounds of Fairham Estate, and he planned to seek out as many as he was able of those young boys, some whom had not yet attained their twentieth birthday, and find a way to pull them back from their despair. To give them a future. To give them hope.

Now that a plan was in place for her future, Pru was content to wait a while before making it known to the Channings. The announcement of Emily and Charles's betrothal had been sent to *The Morning Post* and arrangements were already under way for the wedding. Emily had been out for a few weeks now and no-one saw any reason to delay the happy day.

Pru saw little of Becky in the next few weeks, what with shopping with her cousin for bridal clothes, discussing with Aunt Gussie what refreshments should be offered to their guests and all the other countless details associated with a Society marriage, for Lord and Lady Channing were only too happy to lay down the most lavish arrangements for their eldest daughter. Mrs Standish was not of their set and Augusta saw no reason at all to include her.

One day, when Pru and Becky had managed to snatch a while together in Sydney Gardens, it was decided that Becky should travel into Somerset to see what properties might be available to them. She had, over the years, maintained infrequent correspondence with her old nurse who still lived in the area.

"Jane was ever a romantic soul and disapproved of my parents trying to force me into an arranged marriage. She acted as go-between when Standish and I were meeting secretly. She lives still in a small cottage in the grounds of my former home, my brother not having the heart to cast her upon the world when he came into the property."

"Your brother? But you said…"

"He was up at Oxford at the time of my elopement and I have not seen him since, nor heard from him. I know not what my parents told him or how he felt, but we have been estranged all this time. I must assume I am dead to him so I spoke only the truth, as I saw it, when I said you were my only relative."

Pru hooked her arm through Becky's as they walked, the winter sunshine casting little warmth upon them. Both though were country-bred and their brisk pace did much to alleviate the cold.

"Might there be the opportunity for a reconciliation, do you think?"

"It is possible, I suppose. To tell you the truth, Pru, I would be happy indeed if William desired to meet me."

"But surely he doesn't live in Somerset? Had I an uncle there, of a certainty I should have known."

Becky clutched Pru's arm more tightly and gurgled delightfully. "And so you might, had my parents not argued with your father and cut ties with my sister as well. They were not the most easy-going of creatures and a professional soldier was not what they had planned for Sally, no matter how highly born. And then, when she died, there was no hope or need for a reconciliation. Having been away from home for so long, I suspect William was and is entirely unaware of your existence. Indeed, it's quite possible my parents too were unaware that they had a granddaughter."

Pru, for a moment shocked, responded almost immediately to her aunt's ready laughter. It seemed she was not quite as alone in the world as she had imagined. Her excitement mounted. "I cannot wait to leave Bath and discover what I may about my mother's family. Do go, Becky. Stay with Jane. Find us a house if you can. I will join you in a few weeks and, if your Jane cannot accommodate me also, I have friends with whom I can stay until we can be settled. What a thrilling time we have in front of us!" she exclaimed, twirling her aunt around to the astonishment of nearby onlookers.

Becky wasted no time, waiting only for a reply to her letter to the trusty Jane that of course she would be welcome and may stay as long as she pleased. It was fortunate that Aunt Gussie, taken up with her eldest daughter's forthcoming nuptials, made only a token effort to sway Pru from her decision. Still, as she said to her husband, "What is the point of wasting my breath when her mind is made up, Edward? I only pray she is not making the biggest mistake of her life. Her father was just as stubborn. While I cannot be glad that she is to reside with Mrs Standish, it is better by far than her former plan of setting up on her own with no-one to give her countenance."

Lord Channing forbore to tell his wife that it was really none of her concern. Prudence was of age and might do as she wished. He liked her immensely and had always been happy to welcome her into his home, but that she should reside with them on a permanent basis was not the solution for an independent young woman such as she was. His niece was a woman as capable as she was charming, and he desired nothing but happiness for her.

Pru remained in Bath for a further two weeks after her cousin's wedding. She was well aware that Gussie, with her two younger girls not yet out of the schoolroom, would be missing Emily, and that to remove herself at the same time seemed to Prudence to be unnecessarily cruel. Lady Channing would in time become accustomed to her altered state, but she ventured out less frequently on these long winter evenings. Instead she enjoyed nothing more than a comfortable conversation in front of the fire, going over again and again the details of Emily's dress and how kind the weather had been on the day of the wedding. Pru bore her outpourings with patience, but when she received a letter from Becky asking her to come as soon as may be, she judged it to be time to leave.

Fortunately, the young couple had returned from their honeymoon and Mrs Wrotham visited her mama on the morning before Pru's departure. Her husband accompanied her and, when the opportunity arose, he asked Prudence if she'd had word of Captain Staveley. "Do tell him he is welcome to stay with us any time he visits Bath."

That she might be seeing Jack in the near future was something Pru had been anticipating for, with her relocation back to Somerset, nothing was more certain than that they would move in the same circles. "I will be sure to do so," she told Charles.

CHAPTER SEVEN

Prudence departed early the next morning, taking her leave of her aunt, who shed tears and begged her to visit again soon, of her uncle, who kissed her on both cheeks, and of her two younger cousins, both of whom looked upon her as an older sister. Sitting opposite her in the coach, Kitty seemed to be by far the more excited of the two, but Pru was accustomed to disguising her feelings. Beneath her calm exterior the blood was racing through her veins, for a whole new chapter of her life was about to unfold before her. There was a more than usual brilliance in her sapphire eyes. Her uncle had been good enough to offer her the use of his carriage, and it was anticipated that they would cover the journey comfortably in one day, Wells being some forty miles from Bath and Lord Channing's coach well-sprung and his horses good goers.

"How kind of your uncle to provide blankets for us both," Kitty remarked, snuggling deep into the folds of the one that covered her knees and holding its edge up to her chin.

Pru laughed out loud. "What a poor creature you are, Kitty. It is a glorious morning."

"It is, miss, but I do feel the cold something awful."

Pru removed a hand from her muff and wiped away the mist on the window with gloved fingers. Sunlight sparkled off the frost that lay everywhere, giving the whole a touch of magic, but it promised to be a fine day. "The sun is rising quickly now and look, we are almost out of Bath and will soon be travelling through the countryside. I must say, Kitty, I much prefer to be away from town. You must be looking forward to seeing your parents again after so long."

"Fit to burst, miss. Ma writes that my sister has grown so much that I won't know her when I see her again. Will you be visiting Fairham Manor yourself, Miss Prudence?"

Conversation between the two was comfortable for, despite their different stations, the two had grown up in almost daily contact, though naturally certain conventions were observed. However, Pru was unsure of how to answer Kitty's question, for she did not know herself. Her reply was non-committal and she turned the conversation to their immediate destination, which lay only some three miles from her former home, both establishments being a similar distance from Wells, the city in closest proximity.

"We must first settle ourselves with my aunt's old nurse, who has been kind enough to offer us accommodation until we have purchased our new home. I have never visited Wexford Hall, but I understand from Mrs Standish that the grounds are very beautiful and Jane's cottage quite capacious. Once we are established there I will be happy to send you to Fairham Manor in a gig, and I'm sure I can spare you for a few days if you wish to make an extended stay with your family. I make no doubt they would be happy for you to remain with them a while."

As the day warmed, the frost melted and the sun dispelled any residual mist. The view filled both women with a feeling of well-being. It was a perfect day and though they could not hear the birds singing, all other noises being masked by the pounding of the horses' hooves, that was in itself a comforting sound and reassuring in its regularity. They drove past fields and meadows where cows were grazing and sheep could be seen in the distance. Pru had pulled the window down a little and all at once the smell of woodsmoke pervaded the atmosphere.

"Now I know I am back in the country," she declared happily. She leaned back in her seat and relaxed until the rhythm of the horses' movement changed and they pulled into the courtyard of an inn. Bringing his team to a halt, the coachman jumped down and opened the door for the ladies.

"Your uncle desired me to stop here, miss, so you could take refreshment and stretch your legs. If you would be happy to remain for half an hour, I am sure there will be no need to change horses. The master is content for them to complete the journey and return tomorrow when they have rested."

"How very thoughtful of him, Walter. Do please convey my thanks when you next see him," Pru said, alighting from the carriage and smiling warmly at him. While the groom saw to the animals, the landlord showed Pru and Kitty to a small private room where his wife provided them with some very welcome tea after which they took a turn about the garden. Much revived, they went once more to the yard where all was ready for their departure. Prudence found her excitement mounting as, after sitting with her abigail for some while in companionable silence, familiar scenery came into view and she knew she was close to home. She looked again from the window in the direction of Fairham Manor, too much hidden behind a small wood to be visible but very much close at hand. Their own destination was some few miles further on but, just as Pru settled back once more against the cushions, she was hurled across the coach almost into Kitty's lap.

"Good heavens, what can have happened?" the girl asked, a note of panic in her voice as they came to an abrupt halt. Pru, brushing the folds of her dress down and patting at wisps of hair that had escaped her bonnet, said that of a certainty they had hit a hole in the road. Their conveyance was sitting at a strange angle, one corner at the front dipping lower than the rest. As she spoke, the door was pulled open and Walter, all contrition, made haste to explain that one of the wheels had caught a deep hole and was now off its axle.

"Jed is at the horses' heads, them being a bit spooked, but he has 'em under control. I fear it will be some time before we can be on our way again. Would you like to wait in the carriage while we do what we can to fix it, Miss Prudence?"

"No, I would not, for I feel as though I am on the high seas, sitting at such an angle. I shall step down. Come, Kitty, don't distress yourself. I'm sure Walter will have all to rights soon."

Standing on the roadside, Pru was better able to review the damage. She looked at the coachman, one eyebrow raised in query. "I see the damage is worse than I had anticipated, Walter. I am so mortified after my uncle's kindness in lending me his coach."

"He will hardly blame you for the condition of the road, miss."

"No, and at least his horses are unhurt. That would have been dreadful indeed. Well, I must think what is best to do. This is not a matter of a few minutes, or even only an hour. Kitty," she said, turning to her abigail, "I fear we shall have to go to Fairham to enlist their help. It's only a short walk from here and the weather is fine." Turning back to the coachman, she continued, "Stay here with Jed, if you will. We cannot leave him alone to look after my uncle's team and the coach. I will bring aid, or most likely send someone, for I am as sure as I can be that Captain Staveley will himself convey us to our destination. Between us we will decide how the luggage is to be moved. Right, Kitty, let us be on our way. It seems you will be seeing your family sooner than either of us had anticipated."

It was not for Kitty to know the state of turmoil in which Prudence now found herself. Hidden inside her muff, her hands were trembling. The home she had left so many months ago would soon come into view. Only it wasn't her home any longer. The prospect of returning now filled her with dread. Telling herself she was no longer a young girl and making a supreme effort to control her emotions, she moved forward, apprehension and determination occupying her in equal measure.

As luck would have it, Jack was not in the house when they arrived. Pru didn't know whether to be disappointed or relieved, but she put both emotions aside as she explained to Bunting what had happened, having first sent Kitty off in search of her mother.

"Near old Arthur's field, you say? I'll send someone in the gig so they can bring your luggage back here, Miss Prudence. Such a pity you can't stay. Now you're here it seems a shame for you to have to move on."

Pru found that her throat was constricted by a rather large lump but managed to respond. "Thank you, Bunting, it's good of you to say so, but I must be leaving soon. My aunt is expecting me and will doubtless be concerned if I don't arrive as promised."

He tried again, though he knew it to be useless. "We could send a message."

"No. It's kind of you, but no. You know how independent I am, old friend, for have we not crossed swords in the past?"

"What, like the time you took Lightning Flash out on your own with never a thought for your safety, not to mention his?"

"How cross you were with me. And the only way I could mollify you was to assure you I was capable because I had been taught to ride by no less master than yourself."

"Yes, you were always good at cutting a wheedle, even when you were a little 'un."

Pru judged it was time to ask about Jack. "Is Captain Staveley away from home at the moment?" she said as casually as she was able.

"No, he is about the estate somewhere. I dare say he will be back soon."

She received this piece of information as calmly as she could, grateful in a way that the new incumbent was not around. When he had not returned some two hours later and the luggage had been retrieved and loaded onto the gig, she took her leave. She paused only to ask that a message be sent to inform her that her uncle's equipage was repaired and his horses stabled for the night so she could rest easy on that score. Leaving Kitty behind, for she judged it would be cruel to remove her so soon from her family, she left in time to arrive at her destination just as the light was fading. She found Becky in a state of anxiety, not knowing what had delayed her.

"Come in, child, come in. I've been looking for you these two or three hours past. But what's this? How is it that you're arriving in a gig?"

"It's a long story, Becky, and I would put off my hat and gloves before I begin to tell you."

"Of course, but come first and meet Jane. You will love her, I know." Becky took Pru's hand and fairly pulled her into the cottage. The groom had deposited her trunk and several boxes in the hallway and gone on his way. "Don't worry about your luggage. Simon will take it to your room presently."

"Simon?"

"Jane's great-nephew who lives with her here. She's not as strong as she was and he looks after her. They have a cow and some chickens and a vegetable garden, so they are pretty self-sufficient. Ah, here is Jane now," she said as they entered the kitchen and she introduced the two.

Pru put out her hand but Jane, rubbing her own on her pinafore, declined to take it, saying, "You'll forgive me, miss, but mine do be covered in flour for I'm making bread. It be a pleasure to welcome you, Miss Rebecca having told me so much about you. We keep a modest home here, but I trust as you'll be comfortable until such time as you find a place of your own. Though you're welcome to stay as long as you like."

Pru thanked her very prettily and excused herself so she might remove her pelisse as well as her bonnet and gloves, which she had left on a small table in the hall. Her luggage was no longer there and a young man whom she presumed to be Simon was coming down the stairs.

"Good day, miss. I've taken everything up, and there's a bowl of water and a jug should you need them."

"That's very thoughtful of you, Simon. Indeed I would like to freshen up. Will you come with me, Becky?" Pru said, turning to her aunt.

"Indeed I shall, for we have time for a quiet chat before Jane lays the table. I just hope you have a good appetite after your journey, for nothing is more certain than that you won't go hungry in this house."

They had by this time reached the bedchamber that had been allocated to Prudence, and she was delighted. Pretty curtains hung at the window which overlooked the rolling countryside. The room was tastefully furnished and her trunk stood in the corner, waiting to be unpacked. There was a dresser on which stood the bowl and jug that Simon had promised, and she availed herself of them while Becky sat on a chair watching her. Dabbing her face with a towel and feeling much refreshed, she turned to her aunt. "I see no sign of decrepitude in your old nurse, in spite of what you said earlier."

"No indeed, but that's because you didn't know her before. She could never sit still for two minutes at a time and always had to be doing. That hasn't changed and she would be mortified if I suggested to her that she might slow down a little, but it's Simon who does the manual work. It doesn't stop Jane making cheese and baking bread and, oh, all manner of things in the kitchen. I think maybe she had been better suited to be a cook than a nurse, but I'm so grateful that wasn't the case for she has always been such a support to me."

Prudence outlined the events of the day and explained how they had ended up at her old home. "So in the end I decided to leave Kitty at Fairham, for it would have been unkind of me to drag her away from her family so soon," she said, standing at the window and wishing that she herself had not had to be dragged away. "Tell me what has been happening here since last I received a letter from you."

"I shall, but not just yet. For now, let us go down and eat. My maid will empty your trunk and see to your needs as well as mine until Kitty returns to you. You must be hungry, and Jane will be put out if we do not appear at the table soon. One thing before we go down, Prudence. Jane has insisted I eat in the small room she uses as a dining room, while she and Simon use the kitchen. She sets a great deal of store by convention and believes it wrong that we should share a table. Even though I protested that it is her home, she would have no truck with my objections. And so I have accepted the situation, though I feel badly about it, for it would distress her if I argued further, and I would beg that you do the same."

"I must be guided by you in this, of course, but I feel already that I am imposing on her hospitality as she doesn't even know me."

The laugh that Prudence remembered so well and had missed so much in recent weeks pealed out again. "Well, I wish you luck if you choose to object, for I would set my old nurse against anyone in an argument. Even you."

"In that case, let us go down now, for I am famished."

There was little conversation over dinner, but after the covers had been removed Prudence and Becky sat down in Jane's comfortable parlour to talk about their future.

"Tell me quickly everything that has happened since you've been here, for I shall soon fall asleep in this chair," said Pru.

"Then I shall tell you very little until tomorrow, for you will not want it in patches. Suffice it to say that I have not yet encountered my brother, whom I understand to be away on a prolonged visit to Leicestershire, and that I have three properties I would have you inspect, any of which I think might suit our purposes. For the rest, go to bed and we will talk again in the morning."

CHAPTER EIGHT

The good mood that Jack brought home with him from his afternoon exertions turned to one of intense disappointment when he learned that not only had Prudence visited Fairham Manor in his absence but that she had not waited for his return. He had been investigating with Simpkins which site would best suit his forthcoming venture. They had chosen an area where a stream skirted the field and the land was fairly flat on which to build a small hospital and refuge for wounded and disabled soldiers. Having made their choice after several attempts to find the perfect spot, both found they had worked up a decent thirst and rode together to a nearby inn for some well-earned refreshment. And there they sat talking before a welcoming fire, which the host kept replenishing from a pile of logs that stood to the side of it. Simpkins' enthusiasm for the project matched that of his employer, and he couldn't help but remark, "I know that Miss Fairham did her very best all those years the major was away," he confided in Jack. "We talked long and often but there was little we could do, there not being the funds available."

"I make no bones about the fact that I am a very wealthy man, since you are well aware of my circumstances. It is no credit to me, for it is inherited wealth, but I would see others less fortunate benefit from my good luck, Simpkins. As for the estate itself, while not vast, it is of a reasonable size and from all that you have shown me would do very well for being brought back into good order."

The words were music to the steward's ears. A local man, he had been delighted when the major had entrusted him with

Fairham Manor's upkeep, absent as he was for so much of the time, but his delight had turned to frustration, for there was so much unfulfilled potential. Now it seemed he would be given almost free rein to bring up to scratch the place which he regarded as his second home. Work on the estate had already begun, for the captain had not been idle since taking up residence. But this new venture filled both with a passion, each wishing in his own way to render what aid they could to those who had given so much for their country.

The two men parted company and Jack rode back to Fairham Manor with ideas aplenty whirling around in his head. Having stabled Storm, he entered the house through a back door and the first person he saw, carrying a bundle of linen for her mother, was Kitty. She dropped him a curtsey as best she could with her burden and would have moved on but he stopped her, curious to know why she was there and even more interested to discover the whereabouts of her mistress.

"Miss Prudence has gone to her aunt, sir. After the accident she was kind enough to allow me to remain here with my folks for a few days."

"Accident!" Jack said sharply. "What accident?"

"You'd best ask Mr Bunting, Captain. It was he got it all sorted and sent Miss Pru off to Wexford Hall Cottage an hour or two since."

"Was anyone hurt?" he asked anxiously.

"No, sir, not even the horses, though the carriage didn't come off too well as I understand it."

Relieved to know Pru had suffered no injury, he let the girl go and went in search of his old batman. Bunting was able to fill in the details and to explain that the horses were being stabled nearby and the carriage undergoing repairs.

"And Pru? She came here?"

"Yes, for the accident happened close by and, rather than wait on the road, she and Kitty walked through the wood to the house. She stayed a while, but once her luggage arrived and she was assured her uncle's coach and horses were being taken care of she was eager to be on her way, it being late and her aunt expecting her."

"Surely she could have stayed here and travelled on tomorrow," Jack said, the irritation evident in his voice. "A message could have been sent to Mrs Standish."

"I said as much myself, sir, but there was no holding her."

"Did she leave no word for me?"

"She asked only that her conveyance be restored to Lord Channing, together with his horses, as soon as it was reasonable to do so."

Jack ran his fingers through his hair and walked off without another word. Bunting stood for a moment, wondering if there was ever going to be a way of getting the two of them to resume the ease of their earlier relationship.

Sitting down to eat a late supper with very little appetite, Jack couldn't rid himself of the knowledge that Pru was but a few miles away, so near but, under the circumstances, she might just as well still have been in Bath. Leaning back in his chair, he was nibbling at a piece of cheese in a somewhat desultory manner when it occurred to him that he had every excuse to ride over the next day to reassure her. He had, upon crossing to the dining room, received a message from Walter to say all was well and he would be returning home early the next morning. Feeling much happier to have a legitimate reason, but nonetheless apprehensive, he went to bed to dream of wounded soldiers and of Pru moving from one to another, tending to their injuries and adjuring them to practise on their crutches or to learn to do things with their less dominant hand, the other having been lost to them.

He awoke little refreshed but anxious to be on his way. Common sense told him that Prudence may well have been affected by a visit to her old home and that perhaps she might need some time to accustom herself to her new surroundings. However, he was eager to see her again and decided not to postpone his visit. Nonetheless, it would have been inappropriate for him to arrive immediately after breakfast so he bided his time before riding Storm at a steady trot as he pondered upon his disturbed night. This in turn led him to wonder if she would be willing to aid him in his new scheme. Could what he'd dreamed become a reality?

Pru had slept more soundly than she had for many a day, undisturbed by the ceaseless sounds that attended living in a city and only waking with a start to a gentle tap on her door.

"Come in."

"What a sleepyhead you are," Becky said. "I would not have disturbed you now, but there are things we must do. I shall send my maid to you for, as you can see, I am already up and fully dressed. I am so excited about … but no, I'm delaying you. I will tell you over breakfast. It's so lovely to have you here, my dear."

With Martha's help, Pru was ready in no time and joined her aunt downstairs. Jane entered the room with some fresh milk, giving her guest an opportunity to express her gratitude. "I cannot remember when last I slept so well. It is good to be back in the country, and I cannot thank you enough for accommodating me."

"Now, don't you talk such nonsense, miss. You be welcome to stay as long as you like."

Becky joined in the conversation, adding, "That may well be less time than any of us anticipated, Jane, for I am taking Miss Prudence to see those houses I told you about. All three are standing empty so, if one of them should prove to suit, there will be no bar to us moving in quite quickly." She turned to her niece as the older woman left the room. "That is why I needed to wake you this morning. The agent is to meet us at the first and then escort us to the other two. I have hired a gig as I do not keep my own horses yet, for there is no facility to stable them here, but I cannot wait until we are settled and able to drive out together."

"It's fortunate you didn't tell me this last night, or I might not have slept through the excitement," Pru replied. "Are they all of a size, these houses?"

"None is large, but neither are they too small for us to entertain. As well as a dining room each has a library and a large sitting room in addition to a small morning room. And I believe there are one or two other rooms also. There are several bedrooms, and —" Becky paused for effect, her eyes round and glistening with fun — "all three boast a ballroom!"

Pru laughed aloud. "You are planning that we shall be entertaining on the grand scale?"

"Who knows what we might do? It is better to be prepared, just in case. Come now, finish your breakfast, for we must leave soon."

Half an hour later the ladies set off, the gig having been kept waiting only some ten minutes after the allotted time, the younger taking the reins while the older gave directions.

Daventry House was some three miles distant. The agent, a Mr Tolley, was waiting for them and began to guide them around the property, highlighting its suitability for two women who were to reside together. "You will see that there are several reception rooms, should you each wish to entertain separately. Outside there is sufficient stabling for a good number of horses and carriages, though some refurbishment would be necessary. There is ample room to accommodate visitors, a well-developed kitchen garden and a terrace leading from the ballroom to grounds which have been maintained to a high degree."

"Perhaps we may see the ballroom next?" Pru asked, trying and failing to curb the bubble of anticipation that was growing ever larger. Becky took her arm and squeezed it, thus demonstrating her own enthusiasm. It was judged, all in all, to be a very suitable place though there was a deal of decorating to be done and, of course, furniture to be purchased. Had they not arranged to see two more, Prudence and Becky would in all probability have decided there and then to take it but, mounting the gig, they followed Mr Trolley for another two miles to a property that Pru was familiar with.

"Why, is this not the home of the Armitage family?" she asked.

"It is indeed. I take it you've been here before, Miss Fairham."

"I have, many years ago. Have they been long gone, do you know?"

"I believe Mr Armitage passed away a few months ago and his widow went to live with her daughter. There was no sense, she said, in keeping the house because it held so many memories she felt she would never be able to bring herself to return."

Pru knew all about memories and was conscious of how painful it had been to visit Fairham Manor on the previous day. "It was on account of Miss Armitage that I visited. I remember now that she was married and went with her husband into Sussex, I believe."

"That's correct. It's probable, then, that you know the house better than I do but we will continue, if you please, for the benefit of Mrs Standish."

"Oh, I never saw it all before and I should like to inspect the whole."

Set in the grounds of a large landscaped garden with a small copse at its rear, it was eminently suitable in a lot of respects but did not have enough land attached to satisfy either lady. With their thoughts returning to the first, they agreed immediately that it would not do for them.

The third property was another that Pru knew well but one whose boundary ran with that of Fairham Manor, and she could not contemplate living in such close proximity with her former home. Becky could see that she was distressed and suggested they leave without going inside, something Pru was happy to do. Neither lady had any doubts about Daventry House and decided without any more hesitation to go ahead with signing the lease. Mr Tolley promised to have the necessary paperwork prepared for their man of business to inspect and to organise such staff as they might require. They parted company and the ladies returned to Wexford Hall Cottage, the day by this time being well advanced and both being ready for the late lunch that Jane had waiting for them.

"A young gentleman came by to see you, Miss Fairham. Seemed right put out when you weren't here. Asked when you might be back but I told him I didn't rightly know, so he said he wouldn't wait and left his calling card."

Pru didn't need to see the card to know that it was Jack who had called. It seemed they were destined to keep missing each other.

CHAPTER NINE

Jack had to swallow his setback as best he could, regretting the tactics that had made him wait before riding over to Wexford Hall. No matter how much he told himself that his visit would of necessity have been curtailed if the ladies were expected elsewhere, a short visit would have been preferable to none at all. He'd given no thought as to what he would do with the rest of his day, having focused all his attention on seeing Prudence again.

Returning to Fairham Manor, he paused only to change his clothes before taking out his gun and going hunting. He found no sport but the exercise served to calm his agitation and he resolved to call on Prudence the next day and, if necessary, every day until he was successful. In the meantime, he thought it would do him no harm to study the plans he had discussed with Simpkins. This served him so well that he lost all track of time and had to be summoned for supper. One or two glasses of port soothed him further and he fell into a dreamless sleep, thankful that the demons that so often haunted his nights were for once kept in abeyance.

The next morning it could be seen that the crisp sunny winter days they had been enjoying were at an end. Rain fell monotonously from a grey sky and would, under other circumstances, have kept Jack at Fairham Manor. He had, however, engaged to visit one of the tenant farmers to discuss the damaged dry stone walls which were failing to keep his livestock enclosed. Reparations would be costly and time-consuming. For many years things on the estate had not been run with any great degree of efficiency. Jack had promised to make an inspection and, if he deemed it necessary, to contribute to the restoration, either by providing the required labour or affording funds so that the farmer could himself hire someone to do the work. It was Jack's hope that, once the Fairham Manor estate had been restored to a long ago former glory, there would be increased productivity, a benefit both to himself and his tenants. To this end he was prepared to invest some of his exceedingly large fortune into the land. Somewhere in a corner of his mind was also the thought that he would be honouring the man who had been like a father to him.

As owner of the estate he could have made some excuse to delay his visit to Puddlestone Farm, but Jack was not one to stand on his dignity or go back on his word. Donning his hat and a many caped cloak, he set out on Storm soon after breakfast. He was amused to think that he might indeed find many puddles at his destination, though insufficient stone. As the rain beat down he reflected too that the name Storm well suited his horse in the present weather conditions. Even the torrent could not dampen Jack's spirits. For one thing, as a soldier he was used to being out in all weathers and had learned over the years either to disregard or ignore its eccentricities. For another, Puddlestone Farm lay in the direction of Wexford Hall Cottage and gave him an excuse, should he feel the need of one, to call upon Pru.

"It's right good of you to come out in this weather, sir," said Albert, the tenant farmer, after Jack had dismounted and tethered his horse. "Everywhere the dust has turned to mud and it ain't a pleasant day, not at all."

"Then we will deal with our business as swiftly as we may and I shall leave you to get on with it," Jack replied, slapping the man good-naturedly on the shoulder. Albert's wife insisted on providing some refreshment before the men set out and the landlord was well able to see that the neglect was in no way due to a lack of will on the part of the tenant but more to the ravages of time, a long period of time, when carelessness or indifference had led to the current state of affairs. Jack agreed to pay Albert to hire some labour and materials and left the farm, both men being satisfied at the outcome. The captain looked down at his drenched self, in two minds as to whether or not to continue on to the cottage in the grounds of Wexford Hall. Satisfied that beneath his hat and cloak he was presentable enough, and loth to relinquish the opportunity, he mounted again and proceeded at a trot in the direction, he hoped, of Miss Prudence Fairham. The rain having abated, he was able to spot a small patch of blue in the sky and hoped it was a sign that he would find his quarry at home.

"There's a gentleman here to see you, miss," Simon said, having tapped gently on the door and popped his head around it on being asked to come in. "Captain Staveley what called the other day."

"Please show him in, Simon," Pru said, nervous of seeing Jack after all that had passed between them in recent months. Both she and Becky rose as he came into the room and Becky was the first to move forward in greeting.

"How delightful to see you again, Captain Staveley. It seems an age since last we met, when you sent me to Bath to meet Prudence."

"Indeed it does. How are you? And you, Pru? You have managed to escape the clutches of Lady Channing, I see," he said, a smile lighting his handsome features.

"You are too harsh, Jack," she replied, though her smile matched his and she began to relax a little. "My aunt was very good to me, but live with her forever I could not." They clasped hands in greeting and might, had she not intervened, have forgotten that Becky was in the room, seated again and watching them with interest.

"Yet you are prepared to live with *this* aunt. I hope you will not find after time that you feel the same way about me," Becky said, her infectious laugh ringing out. "You must know that Pru and I are to set up home together. Only yesterday we found what we hope will be the perfect property for us and even now the agent is dealing with the details. Do sit down, Captain. If I know Jane she will be bringing in some refreshment at any moment."

Jack released Pru's hands and she asked what had brought him out on such an inclement day. He was glad to have a ready answer, which caused her to exclaim, "Surely you must be soaked to the skin?"

"Not I, though I suspect that my cloak and hat will take a long time to dry out. I have left them outside in the hall and must apologise to Jane, for I am sure they are dripping all over her floor. I had promised to visit Albert, as he is having a problem which I said I would look into. It would have been churlish of me not to have gone just because of a little rain."

"Little rain!" Becky exclaimed.

"I have known far worse in the field. So tell me about this new place of yours. Does it lie far from here?"

"It is Daventry House. Only some three or so miles from here. Do you know it?" she asked.

"I do not, Mrs Standish, but I'm very much still learning my way around."

Silence fell as all three realised the implication. It was Staveley who was now living at Fairham Manor and it was his doing that had necessitated Prudence leaving her childhood home, though of this latter Becky was unaware. He could have kicked himself for being so gauche but it was Pru who was the first to speak, quick to fill an awkward gap. She no longer blamed Jack but that didn't make the situation any less painful. "Well, it isn't a place I knew of before yesterday either, but it will suit us admirably, I believe. There is some redecorating we would wish to do but the house itself is solid and —" she paused, looking at her aunt with a gleam in her eyes — "there is a ballroom. We are determined to be full of gaiety and plan to hold lots of parties once we are settled in."

"We shall be dissipated beyond belief."

"Then I hope very much that I shall be invited to take part in this dissipation, for it is some time now since I have attended any sort of party."

"Yours, then, will be the first invitation we issue. Ah, here is Jane. Thank you. If you would but set it down there, I will pour. Miss Fairham and I are full of hope that you will continue to bake for us, Jane, even when we are no longer living here, for nobody makes cakes as well as my old nurse."

"Never mind your cajoling, Miss Rebecca. A plain cook I am and a plain cook I will always be. I can't be doing with all that fancy stuff," she said, scuttling out of the room again.

"How are your own plans progressing, Jack? You mentioned that you are investing in Fairham Manor in an effort to restore it to its former glory," Pru said in an effort to set him at his ease.

"Visiting Albert today was just part of that. There is much to be done, as well you know, and you have in Simpkins a man who loves the place as if it were his own. He has been so helpful in formulating schemes. But there is more," he replied, warming to his subject. "You are well enough acquainted with me to know it is against my nature to be idle for long. I have had an idea."

He said this with all the drama anyone could have wished, and he was not disappointed at the response from either lady. Becky, in the process of handing him a cup of tea, looked wide-eyed and questioning while Pru said eagerly, "What is it? I cannot imagine what else you might be doing."

There had been many times in the past when both Jack and Angus had discussed with Prudence the ravages of the battlefield and the plight of the wounded. She was not missish and had always liked it to be told as it was. Now, when Jack told her of this new scheme, she could only stare in admiration and wonder.

"What an excellent plan. I hope I don't have to say that if there's any way I can assist, I would be happy to do so."

Jack was elated. Maybe his dream of Pru tending to the wounded had not been so far-fetched after all.

Though the skies remained leaden, once the rain had abated it did not return. The next week saw Prudence and Becky making almost daily visits to Wells, where they took great pleasure in buying furniture to replace some of the pieces in Daventry House which did not appeal to them. When they did remain at home, it was to pore over samples of wallpaper or hangings which might liven up some of the darker rooms. They derived no little enjoyment from the whole process, each finding in the other an unexpected flair for design.

While she had remained at Wexford Hall Cottage, Prudence was only too aware of the proximity of Fairham Manor. Between visits to Wells and generally preparing to move to Daventry House, and in response to several more visits from Captain Staveley, Pru had gathered her courage and paid a return visit to her family home. Jack had decided to take a chance after Prudence had seemingly fallen into their old way of friendship and he had hopes of seeing her far more frequently now she was back in Somerset. Thus it was on his third visit to Wexford Hall Cottage that he entreated her to return with him to inspect the plans for the proposed refuge. "You have shown such interest and I know you would wish to be part of it all," he said, more in hope than expectation. But he had not been wrong. What better honour could they pay her father's memory than to create a more positive future for those in need? She so strongly felt the need to be involved that, if Jack had not asked it of her, she would herself have put forward the suggestion.

Pru did not return with him on that occasion but he had come to collect her one morning and, as he handed her into the carriage, she was astonished to discover how disturbed she was at his touch. Pushing the sensation to one side she immediately began to talk of the project, channelling her thoughts in a direction other than their close proximity.

"It was good of you to come and collect me, Jack. It has been borne upon me how urgently I need to set up my own stable so that Becky and I will have use of a carriage and I may ride around the neighbourhood as I used to."

"Of course! I don't know why I didn't think of it before, but Firefly, whom you were used to ride when you were at Fairham, is still there and I shall see she is sent to you as soon as you are ready."

"I cannot take your horse," she protested.

"Don't be foolish, Pru," he said forcibly. "You are making something out of nothing. Firefly was always yours, and the sooner you are reunited with her the better." This was the Jack she remembered. Masterful and intolerant of absurdities such as he perceived her objection to be. "And perhaps you will allow me to escort you when looking for a suitable carriage."

Pru opened her mouth to protest but then realised that this too was foolish. It would be much easier if she accepted Jack's help, and the truth was that she would be glad to do so. "That is kind of you. I shall also require a gig to tool around locally. I don't know what Becky may wish. I will discuss it with her and perhaps you may be in a position to help us both."

They arrived at Fairham Manor each filled with eager anticipation, and Pru with no little trepidation. She needn't have worried. While it was no longer her home, she had no cause to feel like an intruder. It so happened that Bunting was in the stable yard when they drove in, and his welcome left her in no doubt about how pleased he was to see her again. It was impossible for Pru to stand on her dignity with one who had known her from childhood and was more in the manner of a beloved uncle than a family retainer. As he helped her down from the carriage, she grasped his hands firmly and leaned forward to plant a kiss upon his cheek.

"Thank you, my old friend, for seeing me safely to my aunt all those weeks ago. And for your aid in ensuring Lord Channing's coach and horses were returned to him in good order. I have received a letter from him since, and all is well."

"It was little enough I could do, Miss Prudence. You know you only need send a message any time if there's some way I can be of assistance."

Jack suggested Prudence might like to visit Firefly in her stall. The reunion was everything she could have wished, and she laughed aloud when her favourite pushed her muzzle into the hand that had always held a piece of apple. Looking around she found that Bunting was holding a piece of fruit which he handed to her and she was thus able to fulfil the ritual. Laying her face against the horse's neck she whispered gently to her, promising the rides they would again have together. Bunting went about his business and Jack left Pru and Firefly alone for a few minutes before she joined him in the yard.

"I must apologise for earlier being so foolish," she said with a smile. "Had you not offered Firefly to me, I must surely have asked. The bond is still there. She has not forgotten me."

"It would be hard to judge which of the two of you showed more delight. Come," he said, "I will show you the plans. They are laid out already in the library and I would value your opinion."

They walked from the stable yard to enter the house by a back door. Kitty was waiting for her. "I heard as how you were coming, Miss Pru, and I came straightaway to see you, to thank you again for allowing me to spend so much time with my folks."

"And I hope you have been making good use of such time for, though it would have been an imposition to bring you to Wexford Hall Cottage, and my aunt's maid has been assisting me, I have been sorely missing you and would have you join me at Daventry House when Mrs Standish and I take up residence. Perhaps you might now bring us some tea in the library," she said, following Jack, and then was suddenly overcome with remorse when she remembered it was no longer her place to give orders in this house.

Not having heard what she'd said, but seeing her discomfiture as the blood rose in her face, Jack asked, "Whatever is wrong, Pru? What has happened to distress you?" She would not say, brushing his questions aside, and he did not press her, but it cast a shadow over them for some moments. It wasn't long, however, before both became immersed in studying the plans, heads together, Jack pointing as he explained the different aspects of the proposed scheme. He brushed her arm as he leaned across the table and she covered her confusion by exclaiming how inspired she was by everything he had set before her. Tea was brought in and they sat down to discuss the project.

"Simpkins throws himself into this with all the enthusiasm I could have hoped for," Jack said, "and has made the whole much easier."

"He did ever have the best interests of the estate at heart. I see the dormitories are arranged in such a way as to give each man a little privacy. That will be of inestimable worth, for they will have much to contend with and everything that can be done for their comfort will be beneficial."

"Perhaps when next you come you would like to inspect the site. It's by the stream, as I told you, and though you know it well I would like to walk it with you. It gave me such a good feeling when I did the same with Simpkins. I knew immediately it was the perfect place."

She could hear his excitement, and her own matched his, but she said, "I fear I will not be able to come again until after Becky and I have moved, which as you know we are planning to do shortly. There is much for us to do before then. I must thank you, though, for including me, for you must know that this is as dear to my heart as I know it is to yours."

"I understand, of course. In the meantime, do tell me when you wish to inspect horses and carriages and I will lay aside the time to take you."

She thanked him and he took her arm and led her back to the carriage. There was little conversation as he drove her home, each being content with the silence.

CHAPTER TEN

In the end it was almost a month after Prudence and Becky had first seen it that they moved into their new home, and Christmas was but a few weeks away. Three days later they received an unexpected visitor. The footman was a good man, for Mr Tolley had chosen well, but with a wooden expression which made the ladies laugh, so obviously conscious was he of his position. He announced that a gentleman had called and had sent up his card. Becky lifted it from the proffered tray and said in astonishment, "William!" and, turning to Larkin, "Good heavens, man, you have surely not left him waiting in the hall. Show him up immediately." As he left the room, she hurriedly explained to Pru that it was none other than her brother. It was evident that she was suffering some trepidation.

"Sit down and calm yourself, Becky. He would not have come had he not wanted to see you."

There was no time for more. The door opened and Larkin announced, "Mr William Colborne, ma'am."

Becky rose again from her chair, as did Prudence. There was no doubting the relationship, for the man who entered the room bore an undeniable resemblance to his sister.

"Well, well, well. So you are my little sister," he said with a smile as expansive as any Becky had ever displayed. "I had thought you abroad still and heard only yesterday that you were back in England and living but a stone's throw away. I hope you don't mind me coming unannounced, but to be honest —" the smile was now without doubt a grin — "I could not resist the temptation of surprising you."

"William. I should have known you anywhere. Mind? I had rather thought you too had cast me out and am therefore delighted to see you. But I am forgetting my manners. Allow me to present to you Miss Prudence Fairham." She paused for effect and her grin now matched his own. "Our niece."

"What's that? One of the Fairhams of Fairham Manor? My niece, do you say?"

"No longer of Fairham Manor. I reside now with my aunt. I am delighted to make your acquaintance, Uncle William," she said, the sparkle in those sapphire eyes giving the lie to the formality of her greeting. "Do please sit down. I will ring for some tea."

"I am sure we all three have some catching up to do," William said. "So you are Sally's daughter. I did not even know she'd had a child. We were estranged from each other, you know. Well, at any rate, my parents had disowned her much as they had Rebecca. I'd been away from home for so long at the time I was unaware of the circumstances. What with boarding at Harrow and then going up to Oxford, where I fancied myself a young buck, I grew apart somewhat from my family. I suppose I just accepted things as they were upon my return. But tell me, Becky, what happened to you?"

If ever two siblings were of the same nature it was William and Rebecca, and the latter immediately shed the nervous anticipation which had accompanied the announcement of her brother's arrival. She told him how she had been swept off her feet by Standish, and how their parents had attempted to force her into marriage with another and that in the end she and her lover had been married by Special Licence and run off to France.

"How very dashing of you. But surely you were under age?"

"You have uncovered my guilty secret, William. I have been less than honest with you. Standish and I were indeed married, but not immediately. Isn't it shocking? It was for that very reason we went abroad. I could not live with him in England under such circumstances, but I can assure you the knot was tied as soon as could be and we were legally married until such time as my gallant husband must needs get himself killed in a duel."

"Well I never. Well I never."

William was lost in thought for a few moments and Prudence looked at Becky in astonishment, for even she had been unaware that her aunt and uncle had lived together before being wed.

"Are you ashamed of me?" Becky asked her tentatively and it was evident she was holding her breath.

"Ashamed? No, I am filled with admiration for your daring and resolve. How in love you must have been, the two of you, and what an adventure. I wish I had known my Uncle Standish."

Becky turned to her brother. "And you, William? Are you ashamed of me?"

"I must tell you, Rebecca, that my recollection of my childhood is of stern parents, neither of whom appeared to have any humour in a single bone of their bodies. I am only amazed that I did not myself run away. But of course the need did not arise. By the time I returned home after my education I was my own man. As for you and Sally, you went and found your own happiness and for that I applaud you."

William remained for an hour, keen to learn as much as he could and to tell them of his own family. He adored his wife, Hester, and was the proud father of two sons and two daughters, the two youngest being still in the schoolroom.

"Bertram and Francis are twins and a more mischievous pair you could not hope to find," he said, obviously content that it should be so. "My parents would not have been able to subdue their spirits as they tried so hard to subdue ours. With term finished and Christmas being upon us, they have returned home for a few weeks, but doubtless they will be off again soon. I hope you can meet them before they go back to university. In fact, why don't you come and spend Christmas with us? I know Hester will be delighted, for she is aware of my visit today and has expressed a wish to see you if you are agreeable."

Prudence looked at Becky, her ready smile showing she was only too happy to accept such an invitation, and so it was agreed.

Prudence and Becky were sitting in the morning room a week later at Daventry House, a spacious saloon which was enhanced by the chosen furnishings. The windows were adorned with luxurious blue hangings, the fabric for which was discovered on a memorable shopping trip when both ladies had simultaneously pointed to the material and exclaimed, "That's it!" The same was chosen to cover the chaise longue and other upholstered pieces and the finished effect satisfied both. It soon became their favourite room, and a fire was set there each day to ward off the chill of the increasingly wintry days. They were discussing the merits of all they had done so far and how much there was yet to do. Pru and Becky had realised, when redecorating their respective bedchamber and dressing room, that it was necessary with so many empty cupboards to embark on another shopping expedition for, as Pru said, "Aside from purchasing new gowns, it is in any case imperative that I order a new riding habit, for once the stables have been refurbished I shall be bringing Firefly here and will resume the daily rides I used to enjoy so much."

"I, on the other hand, though I have never been much in the way of riding, have always enjoyed driving. If Captain Staveley is to aid us in purchasing a team and carriage, I must of course have the necessary ensemble to do it justice."

It had become apparent even when staying with Jane that the two ladies would live together convivially. The discrepancy in their ages seemed to be of no account, for they shared a sense of humour and a degree of independence which made them compatible.

There was, in addition to the morning room, a drawing room, a library, a small dining room, a large dining room and a music room, all of which could serve to accommodate them, should they at any time choose to be private from each other. As for the number of bedchambers, the house boasted far more than they might ever anticipate needing and Prudence could only be grateful that her mother's legacy was sufficiently substantial for her to contribute her share of the cost, for there was no way she would allow herself to become Becky's pensioner.

"The ballroom is coming along well, don't you think, Pru?"

"Indeed it is. We have only to decide whether our first function will be a ball or something smaller. As you are aware, I have a large acquaintance in the neighbourhood, though they are somewhat spread about. I cannot decide if we should invite them all at once or begin with something less ambitious."

"Oh, definitely a ball, I think," Becky replied with enthusiasm. "We shall become all the rage, just you wait and see."

"Outrageous, more like. You are determined to make a splash, I see."

Becky put her head on one side for a moment and her face became serious. "I left under a cloud all those years ago. I would, if I can, return in triumph. Can you understand that, Pru?"

Prudence burst into laughter and said, "Definitely outrageous!" and the smile returned to Becky's face. "But wait," Pru continued with a frown. "We have not considered enough. At this time of year we cannot rely on moonlight. It's not like living in town where one might have the advantage of artificial light. I fear that few would venture out at night in winter and that we must abandon all thoughts of a ball until the spring."

Becky's face was a picture of disappointment which made Pru laugh out loud once again, but she was quick to come up with another scheme.

"How would it be if we held a house party? There would be fewer people, of course, but we have rooms enough for some twenty or more, I am sure."

"What a famous idea. I must rely on you to decide who we shall invite, though I hope William and Hester may be persuaded to attend."

"Of course. We must be prepared also for some of our neighbours to be residing in London for the winter, but I feel certain we can muster enough to make it a squeeze and that, you know, is a sign of success for any party. Oh, Becky, you cannot know how happy I am to be busy again and in control of my own fate."

With all there was to do, it seemed the Christmas visit to Wexford Hall came upon them within the blink of an eye. Their new carriage, purchased with the aid of Captain Staveley, deposited them in front of Becky's old home. She gripped

Pru's hand tightly before descending onto the drive, for the last time she had seen this place she was fleeing from all she had ever known to be with her lover. It was soon to be seen that there was no need for such trepidation. William and Hester, their offspring ranged behind them, moved forward eagerly to welcome their long-lost sister and Prudence, stepping down behind her, could only be glad her aunt had received such a welcome. It took several moments before all introductions were made and Pru, only slightly less apprehensive, was embraced by those members of her family of whose existence she had only recently learned. The Colbornes were not the sort to stand upon ceremony and all entered the house, all talking at once, until Becky paused just inside the large entrance hall and cast her eyes about her. Everyone stepped back to give her room.

"It is exactly as I remember it," she said, clasping her hand to her breast. Whereupon she burst into tears and Hester, shooing her children away, embraced Prudence and told William to take her into the drawing room while she escorted Becky to her old bedchamber.

William stood aside to allow Prudence to pass before him into the room which she found already occupied by all four of her cousins and a man whom she judged to be some thirty years of age. He stood by the fire and upon her entrance raised an eyebrow in a way she found hard to decipher and, though she could not have described it as rude, it made her feel a little uncomfortable. A handsome man, he nonetheless had the appearance of one who was bored and perhaps more than a little arrogant. All this she surmised as he moved forward to be introduced.

"Allow me to present Hugo Bannerman, Hester's younger brother," William said. "He also is staying with us over Christmas."

"Though no doubt you would wish me to go to the devil, eh, William?" Bannerman answered with a smile which so greatly transformed his features that Pru wondered if her first impression had been mistaken. "I'm delighted to make your acquaintance, Miss Fairham. But where is my sister-in-law? Surely she has come with you?"

"Hester has taken her first to her room. No doubt they will be with us shortly. Well, so we are cousins, are we not?" said Prudence, turning to the younger members of the family. "You will have to forgive me, Bertram, and you too, Francis, for I fear it will be some time before I am able to distinguish between you."

"Watch they don't play off their tricks on you, Miss Fairham, as they have with me on many occasions in the past. An abominable pair, to be sure," Bannerman said, showing himself to be a man of considerable charm who, judging by their reaction, was looked upon with some adulation by his nephews. He looked directly at Prudence, and she couldn't help but respond to his smile before turning from him to the two young girls.

"And which is Sophie and which Susan? Forgive me, already I have forgotten."

The taller of the two stepped forward. "I am Sophie and I'm to make my come-out next year," she said with such precocity that her father said she would be banished to the schoolroom if she continued to speak with such a want of delicacy. Put in her place, she pouted and stepped back.

Susan dropped a curtsey, saying, "And I am fifteen and very pleased to meet you, Cousin Prudence."

"So formal, both of you. I would much prefer a hug." Prudence opened her arms and they moved into her embrace.

"I say, Cousin, that's a bang-up turnout you arrived in. I like the look of the bays you have in harness," said Bertram. At least she thought it was Bertram, but the brothers had moved while she was engaged with their sisters so she couldn't be sure.

"Yes, we're delighted with them. Your aunt and I both like to drive, though I prefer to ride. Your father has been kind enough, as we are to be here for several days, to allow me to have my mare, Firefly, brought over."

"Nonsense," said William. "While you remain here I would have you treat my home as your own."

"You are more than generous, Uncle William. I have so been looking forward to this visit. Ah, here are my aunts," Prudence said, looking anxiously at Becky and feeling reassured that she now seemed to be restored to her usual sunny humour. Hugo Bannerman, who had resumed his position by the fire, moved forward to be introduced and then, such was obviously the way with this delightfully informal family, everyone began talking at once. Pru felt a tap on her arm and turned to find Bannerman standing at her elbow.

"Perhaps you will do me the honour of riding with me, Miss Fairham? I am familiar with the estate and could show you around, should you wish."

"I'd be delighted. I'm as curious as the next person and cannot forget that this was my mother's home too, before her marriage. It would give me great pleasure to learn about the place where she spent her childhood."

While the younger girls would normally eat in the schoolroom, William, a man Prudence liked more and more every moment, maintained that it was a family party and that it would be unkind to exclude them. Moreover, the informality continued to the dining room where, instead of the polite custom of speaking only to the persons seated on either side, conversation criss-crossed the table.

Afterwards, nothing would do but for Prudence and Hugo to get down on the floor with the younger members of the family for a game of spillikins, and they had only been playing a short while when Becky could no longer resist the temptation to join them. She proved to be so accomplished that they seriously considered banning her from the next game.

"We have no chance against you, Aunt Becky. How are you able to keep your hand so still? Mine always shakes when it's my turn," said Susan.

"I take a deep breath and focus very hard," Becky answered, thoroughly enjoying herself.

"Well, that doesn't do for me. Every time I try to concentrate my arm goes rigid and will not obey the instructions from my head."

"You must just accept, I think, that my sister is a superior player and hope to come about when we play again. Now I think it's time for you girls to retire," said William.

They went without demur, pausing only to kiss their older relations goodnight while completely ignoring their brothers, as is the way with siblings. Bertram and Francis went off to play billiards and a card table was set up, Hester choosing to sit and watch while the other four played. The luck was with Prudence, but she was disconcerted to see how seriously Bannerman took the game even though the stakes were minimal. It reminded her too much of her father and it was difficult for her to remain outwardly cheerful when she remembered all she had lost.

However, when the cards were put away, Hugo invited her to ride out with him in the morning. "It promises to be a bright and sunny day, if you don't mind the cold."

"Better by far than a deluge," she replied, remembering the day not so long ago that Jack Staveley had ridden over to Wexford Hall Cottage in the pouring rain. "I should be delighted."

Pru woke the next morning eagerly anticipating her ride. She found herself also looking forward to becoming better acquainted with Hugo Bannerman. The man intrigued her. One moment he was aloof and the next all smiles. Today she would learn much more about him, for it was her firmly held belief that you could judge a person by the way they rode and, more so, by how they treated their mount.

With Kitty's aid, Pru donned the new riding habit of which she was justly proud. It was a simple design of blue cloth, the colour of which accentuated the sparkle in her eyes. Trimmed with braid of a slightly darker shade of blue, the whole was topped by a very fashionable hat which boasted a large feather, the tip of which fell forward and to the side at an audacious angle.

The weather had lived up to its promise. As Prudence and Bannerman set out to explore the estate where her mother had been raised, she tried, and failed, to conjure up a vision of the child who had been Sally Colborne and for that she was sad. She was aware, though, that her parent had been as fond of riding as she was herself, for Angus had told her as much. They walked the horses for a while, Hugo suggesting that they might break into a canter when they had cleared the gardens and the drive. She was curious about the man beside her and asked, "Does your own home lie far from here, Mr Bannerman?"

"I have lodgings in London, Miss Fairham. I am happy to say my sire still lives, and resides in Leicestershire but, even were that not the case, I have an older brother who stands to inherit."

She was a little surprised that he had not chosen to spend Christmas at his family seat but made no comment, asking him instead if he liked living in London.

"I would choose to live nowhere else. For me it holds everything I could ever need, and I do not enjoy residing in the country. I am happiest when surrounded by all that the metropolis has to offer." He then answered the question she was burning to ask but was too polite to do so. "You may wonder why I am here now. I am, as they say, on a repairing lease," he said with a smile. "The cards have not been kind to me of late and necessitated me leaving town before I found myself cleaned out entirely. May I say, Miss Fairham, that it gives me considerable pleasure to find you staying at Wexford Hall for, fond as I am of my sister's family, I would not, were my pockets not to let, choose to spend too many days here."

She was flattered at the implication but was nonetheless disappointed at this side of the man who could on the one hand be so charming and on the other so disdainful. She could not make up her mind whether she liked him or not and decided to defer judgement.

They had by this time reached more open ground, and she was pleased when he said, "Time to give them their heads," for she was not entirely comfortable with the conversation. When they reined in a while later, Pru's cheeks were flushed with the exhilaration of a good canter and she was again at one with her host. He had proved to be a clipping rider, giving his mount fulsome praise when they slowed to a walk.

"There is a tenant farmer close by where I have stopped on previous visits. The man is always happy to provide refreshment. Would you care to visit?"

"I should indeed, for I am parched after that. I must thank you, sir, for inviting me to ride out with you as I should have had no clear idea where to go and have thus far enjoyed myself immensely."

"It is to be hoped you will continue to do so," Bannerman said. "And here we are, and we are in luck. Joseph is home. That is he, working on something at the front of the house. Good day to you, Joseph!" He raised his voice to catch the farmer's attention.

Joseph looked up and Prudence could see surprise in his face, though she didn't then understand why. "Do you care to dismount? Alice will be right glad to see you, sir, and the lady. She has been a-baking this morning so no doubt will have something good to offer you."

He led them into the house, where Prudence perceived a similar reaction from his wife. Alice put her hand to her heart and said, "You do be the image of Miss Sally. I make no doubt you must be her daughter, and if that be the case I'm mighty glad to make your acquaintance." Whereupon she pulled out a handkerchief and dabbed her eyes.

"How kind of you, and you are right, of course. My name is Prudence Fairham, but I never had the pleasure of knowing my mother for I was but a small child when she died. Perhaps you might talk to me about her."

"Yes, I surely will, but first sit yourself down, miss, and I'll fetch some cake and something to drink," Alice said, dusting an already perfectly clean chair for her guest before bustling off into the kitchen.

Prudence and Bannerman spent a pleasant hour before continuing their ride. She learned that her mother had been just such an intrepid rider as herself. They'd seen less of William as a child but they were of course by now entirely familiar with him, he being far more connected with his land than Pru's father had been with his. Becky they hardly knew at all because riding had never been for her a favoured pastime, and the farm was situated at some distance from The Hall, as they called it.

"And did you also know my mother, Joseph?"

"Aye, that I did, for we were of a similar age and whenever she came with her father to see mine we would stand a little apart from the rest while they talked of pigs and chickens, stone walls and crops. No matter what the time of year or the season she would beg me to show her what animals were on the farm. More than once we sat in that barn over there, feeding the lambs or milking the cows. Turn her hand to anything, she would, where the livestock were involved."

"Tell me, then, how both you and Alice knew my mother so well, for you cannot, the two of you, have lived on this farm as children."

It was Alice's turn to put herself forward, explaining that though her father worked a parcel of land a little distance away, her mother was employed as a maid up at The Hall and Alice had been permitted to go with her as a girl. "It made me feel right grown up, helping out as I did from time to time, but mostly I used to hang about in the stables and, as Miss Sally was to be found there at every opportunity, like as not we'd get talking, both of us being in the way of caring for the horses."

"And later, when you were grown, did you see her as a young lady, before she married my father?" Prudence asked.

"I surely did, Miss Fairham. It was the horses, you see. And then me and Joseph were so young when we were wed, him having had his eye on me for a while, so she would always come in and pass the time of day with me when she was out riding. I can't credit how much you resemble her. Her hair, if you don't mind me saying, had that same way of curling and escaping her bonnet. Such a fright I caught when you walked through the door, it might have been Miss Sally standing right before me."

Prudence became aware of a constriction in her throat and it was with difficulty that she tore herself away. She left with the sound of Alice begging her to call again so they might talk more.

Judging it best to follow convention during her visit to her uncle and aunt, Prudence had chosen to bring a lady's saddle to Wexford. Before she was aware, Bannerman had grasped her by the waist and lifted her onto Firefly's back. Though she wasn't in any way missish, she was unsure how she felt about being handled in this way. She would normally have mounted on her own, using a block to assist her. Here there was no block and her discomfiture came not from the act, but that it was undertaken without consultation. To have made a fuss would have served no purpose, but she resolved not to be put in a similar position again. She did not like his audacity or the assumption that, unasked, she would welcome his assistance. It put a blot on what had otherwise been a very pleasant morning. When Hugo asked if they might repeat the exercise another day she acquiesced, but secretly resolved either not to dismount or to do so when she might return to the saddle unaided.

CHAPTER ELEVEN

Jack Staveley didn't spend Christmas alone either. At the same time as Pru and Becky were arriving at Wexford Hall, a carriage, piled high with luggage and preceded by two riders, drew up outside Fairham Manor. Rupert Fitzroy dismounted, followed by Oliver Hervey and, upon being shown into the library where the captain was studying some papers, exclaimed, "Hope you don't mind, old chap. Just couldn't face a week with the relations. My brother's there, you know, and if I'd stayed there's no doubt we'd have come to blows. Always do. Hervey was with me, so we took it into our heads to bolt here and visit you instead."

Jack was glad of the company. Prudence and Becky would be remaining with the Colbornes until the new year, and his acquaintance was still sufficiently small that he'd resigned himself to having little more to do than spending time studying the plans for the projected rehabilitation centre. He stood and shook hands warmly with both men.

"A wise move if your family's anything like mine." He was able to joke about it now, but for a long time after the estrangement he'd found it difficult to even think about without regret. "If I know Mrs Jenkins she's already disposing of your luggage."

"Any news of Miss Fairham?" Olly asked cautiously, aware of how different the position was since last he'd seen her.

Jack's response was cheerful, firstly because he'd had considerable contact with Prudence in recent weeks and secondly because, with no way of altering the situation, it seemed to him that the less said about the changes surrounding the circumstances of the major's death the better. "She's settled in a house quite close by and is living with her aunt. It seems to suit them both well."

"Her aunt!" Fitz exclaimed. "I thought she resided in Bath."

"This is another aunt. I believe you've both met her. Rebecca Standish. Used to live abroad. Latterly in Brussels, though I believe they moved around infrequently. Until her husband got himself killed in a duel."

Both men looked astonished. Fitz replied, "Well, I'll be damned! A fine-looking woman as I recall, and an excellent dancer. Stood up with her at a ball once. Devoted to Standish, I thought. How did she take it?"

"Badly, for a while, but I believe she's come to terms with her loss now and is determined to carve out a new life for herself. But come, let's get you some refreshment first and ensure that Cook knows there are two more to cater for. Though, again, I don't doubt Mrs Jenkins will already have done that."

Over dinner, Jack told his friends of his plans for a hospital and rehabilitation centre. Both were full of enthusiasm, and it wasn't too long before talk came around to whether they might be involved.

"You may recall the conversation we had when last we stayed here. About selling out, I mean," Olly said. "Well, I think perhaps the time has come to look to something else. What do you think, Fitz? We could rent somewhere nearby and when the building work is finished we'd be able to help the poor blighters who didn't come home in one piece. We'd understand exactly what they'd been through and that might help them."

Fitz raised his glass and contemplated the contents. "Blood red, this is," he said, swirling the wine around. "I'll never forget some of the things we saw in the war. If there's anything we can do, you can certainly count me in."

Jack rose to his feet and lifted his own glass. "Gentlemen, you would do me a great service, if that is indeed what you wish. But more than that, you would join me in honouring the major's memory. I give you a toast. To Angus Fairham."

"Angus Fairham," the other two repeated.

"And," added, Jack, "let there be no more of this nonsense about renting somewhere. I've been rattling around this place on my own for far too long. I'd be more than happy for you to remain here, if you choose to do so. It's a large house, so there's no call for us to be falling over each other. And to tell the truth…" He paused, sat down and grinned at the other two. "To tell the truth, having spent most of my adult life in service, I'm sick to death of my own company."

The arrival of his friends brought about a change in Jack who, he suddenly realised, had to a degree shut himself away from the rest of the world, so focused was he on the project in hand. He realised that at this time of the year most of the people he knew would already have plans in place and it would be more appropriate to issue invitations for early January, for he was determined that Fairham Manor should once again figure in the community. To that end he, Fitz and Olly sat down to decide what sort of entertainment they might offer.

"Riding always goes down well," the latter said. "I remember when we were last here and the major organised that race. The one where Miss Fairham showed us all the way. It's good hunting land you've got here, Jack."

"And we could have a card party," Fitz added, reducing them all to silence when they recalled the last they had all attended together and the ensuing tragedy.

Jack was the first to pull himself together. "I think it's time also that Cook was given an opportunity to demonstrate his skills. It's been selfish of me to keep his talents all to myself for so long. We shall invite the neighbours to dinner."

"What, all of them?" Fitz exclaimed.

"Why not? However, a quick calculation of numbers suggests that perhaps we should not ask them all at once. So, dinner parties plural. No, not dinner parties but house parties, for we cannot expect that people will travel far at night, not at this time of the year," he said, unknowingly echoing Prudence's concerns about entertaining in the middle of winter. "And, in the meantime, I fear to my shame that I have neglected my tenants. I shall ask Mrs Jenkins to organise some parcels and we will ride out together, the three of us, distributing largesse and the season's greetings in equal measure. It's time, too, that I showed you the site where we're planning to build. What do you say?"

Both men heartily concurred and it was with renewed enthusiasm that all three anticipated the weeks to come.

Over the next few days Fitzroy and Hervey were to discover the extent of the estate, far larger than they had appreciated, and the neglect it had suffered due to lack of husbandry. The several tenant farmers were without exception welcoming and optimistic that help was at last at hand. All had held the major in affection, regardless of his failings as a landlord, but there was hope now on the horizon that conditions would improve. Angus had not bled dry with rents or taxes those who occupied his land but neither had he aided them. "Not since his missus passed away," one man was heard to mutter to his son. "Seemed to lose interest after that."

As they were riding away, Hervey voiced his surprise at Fairham's inattention to his property, so diligent had he been in the welfare of his men. "It seems from what that man said that it all stemmed from when his wife died. Did you ever meet her, Jack?"

"No, never, for that all happened long before I joined up. I believe Prudence was but a small child at the time. In fact I'm sure of it, for she once told me that she has no recollection at all of her mother."

"'Tis no wonder, then, that there was such a bond between her and the major," said Fitz.

They rode on in silence for a while until they came to the place by the river where, Jack explained, the project was to be sited. The other two looked around, both agreeing that it was an ideal situation.

"When does the building start?" Fitz asked.

"The plans are pretty much in the final stages, so there will be no need for delay other than to assemble a team to do the work. You might care to look at them when we return to the manor in case you perceive something that Simpkins and I have missed. I'm keen for work to begin as soon as is practical."

CHAPTER TWELVE

Christmas was past and a new year had begun. Jack and his friends were busy issuing invitations. They were seated at a table in the library and Oliver looked up and across at Jack.

"Do you think Prudence will come to your house party? It must surely raise memories, both good and bad, were she to do so. Might she not be more comfortable declining?"

"I understand your misgivings, Olly, but as she has already expressed a wish to give what aid she can to the rehabilitation centre and that is situated within the estate, I am fairly certain she will attend."

"It's hardly the same, old boy," said Fitz, "for it lies some distance from here."

Jack sat back and looked from one to the other. "Not all that far. Perhaps you underestimate her. I have no doubt she will be prey to conflicting emotions, but she's made of stern stuff and would keep her feelings hidden from the world. In any case, we can but ask. It will be a pity if she chooses not to come, but it is to be hoped she will accept."

"And I am certainly wishful of seeing Mrs Standish again. She'd be an asset to any party, I'd say," Fitz asserted.

"Well, your wish will be granted soon enough, Fitz, for we are all three of us invited to a housewarming luncheon. When I replied, I mentioned that you were both staying here and she insisted I ask you to accompany me."

Oliver, who was particularly delighted as he had developed more than a passing fondness for his erstwhile hostess, said, "Well, it's to be hoped that the weather doesn't throw a rub in the way. When is it to be, Staveley?"

"A week from today. I took the liberty of accepting on your behalf."

"Well, it's a novel idea, a housewarming luncheon. I can see Miss Fairham has anticipated the same problem as we have ourselves, of travelling home in the dark. While I would have no objection, given a full moon, there are, no doubt, some who would prefer daylight hours."

Pleasure was not the only thing that had been occupying Jack's mind. Once the festivities were over, he had again been in contact with Simpkins to discuss their ongoing plans. He was delighted to learn that the manpower was in a fair way to being organised and that they would endeavour to start almost immediately, there being much groundwork to do before any building could begin. It would take longer at this time of year than in a more clement season, for the ground was hard and they were at the mercy of the weather. No-one, however, was keen to brook any delay. Many of the soldiers for whom they were undertaking this project were living in the most difficult of circumstances, and the earlier they began the sooner their misery could be eased. Not that Jack or any of the others were deluding themselves. For some their pain, both physical and of the mind, would continue their whole lives. But rehabilitation was a possibility for many, and to that end the Captain and his cohorts were determined to drive forward with as much speed as possible.

It would have been hard to judge who had most enjoyed the visit to Wexford Hall. Becky had been in a state of emotional turmoil upon arrival but very soon realised that she was more than welcome in her old home. Moreover, she had found in her sister-in-law a woman with a delicious sense of humour and one who was sympathetic to the almost vagabond life Mrs

Standish had led. They spent many happy hours gossiping together while Prudence was out riding with Hugo Bannerman. For Pru, this was the best part of the day. Having formed the intention of keeping him at a distance, she still took pleasure in their daily outings. An entertaining guide and amusing raconteur, he was equally happy to maintain a companionable silence, particularly when mounted, conversation being more difficult in that circumstance. He told her of his life in London and was evidently to be seen on the social scene as well as spending much of his time, he admitted, in the gaming hells where no lady ever set foot. She could not admire this aspect of his life, in the same way as she abhorred the idea of cockfighting and boxing, but she knew them to be a gentleman's occupations and accepted it to be the case.

It wasn't long before Pru realised that Bannerman was making her the object of a mild flirtation. She was convinced this was merely a pleasurable way to pass the time for he knew that, though an independent woman, she was no heiress, and he had asserted quite early on and without compunction that he was on the lookout for a rich wife. He sometimes went a little beyond what was pleasing, but Prudence had no doubt in her ability to hold him in check and it was, meanwhile, a pleasant enough way to pass the time.

When she and Becky returned to Daventry House at the end of their stay, Pru learned without surprise that Hugo Bannerman was to remain in Somerset for a while longer, being quite content to sponge off his brother-in-law while wishing himself elsewhere. It was difficult not to feel disdainful of one who would without conscience so use his relations, and Prudence could only feel a sense of indignation on her uncle's behalf. That said, she didn't feel she could exclude him from her proposed luncheon and he was indeed an asset to any social occasion.

It was a larger than originally anticipated group that assembled on the day at Daventry House. Some two-and-twenty gathered in the dining room just before noon on a cold January morning. It was an informal group and as such Prudence and Becky had prepared no table plan other than that each of them should sit at either end. Bertram was unlucky, he thought, to find himself seated by the squire's wife, until he discovered Mrs Allen was the mother of one of his closest university friends, at present visiting relatives in another part of the country. Well versed in the ways of young men, she very soon sacrificed her son's dignity by repeating several anecdotes of the young Mr Allen's childhood that furnished Bertram with much opportunity for ribbing at a later date. He was happy as well to be introduced to her elder daughter Maria, a girl who engendered in him a desire to protect her, shy as she was. And so began his first calf love. His brother Francis was as yet uninitiated into the ways of budding ladies, his own sisters naturally not, in his mind, coming into that category. He was deep in conversation with the younger Mr Godwin, a near-neighbour who was seated next to him on the other side of the table.

At one end, Becky was amusing William and Hester with an account of the refurbishing of Daventry House. "You will scarcely credit it, but on one occasion I had to climb in through the window!"

Hester laughed. "I wish I might say that I cannot imagine you engaged in such hoydenish behaviour, but the truth is I can, and very easily."

"Well, it was my own fault, of course, for not taking a key. I had been out walking and as I came back through the garden I

114

remembered that Prudence had had the intention of taking Firefly out. There were no staff in the house that morning. They'd been given leave to have some hours away because of the particular work that was being undertaken. It's why I was myself absent." She paused for breath, the smile that rarely left her eyes spreading across her face. "I headed for the door that gave onto the terrace, fully expecting it to give way beneath my hand, but it remained firm in its resistance. I knocked but of course there was no acknowledgement, the builders I thought not deeming it their place to respond and in any case they were working upstairs and may not have heard. I walked around the house, an exercise which took me some time for, as you can see, it is not a small property. Nothing. Nobody. There was only one thing for it. With my reticule swinging on my arm, I hoisted my skirts and climbed in through a window which had been inadvertently but fortuitously left open."

Hester and William both burst out laughing and Prudence looked up from her conversation with Staveley and Hervey to see what was the cause of such merriment. She experienced a feeling of wellbeing as she glanced around, for everyone was engaged in talking and it was apparent that the party was proving to be a great success. Bannerman was seated next to Fanny Lambert, the daughter of another neighbour, and it could be seen that the young woman was hiding her blushes behind her fan. Pru hoped Hugo wasn't overstepping the mark for, even though Fanny was perhaps some twenty years of age and indeed had her parents at hand to protect her, she would have been filled with remorse if he had crossed the line. But just before she looked away she noticed that Miss Lambert had rapped his knuckles playfully with her fan and concluded she was well able to take care of herself. Hervey claimed her attention again, telling her about the progress of the work at

Fairham Manor. Together with Jack, they had talked of little else during the meal. Fitz, seated too far away to participate, was entertaining Maria and Louisa Allen.

The meal over, they adjourned to the drawing room and it was as they walked along the corridor that Becky, looking out of the window, declared, "Oh look, it's snowing. How very pretty."

No-one had noticed, and it was indeed pretty. It was also evident that the snow had been falling hard and fast for some time. Everywhere was covered in a thick layer and there were exclamations of dismay from both Mrs Godwin and Mrs Lambert, though the younger members of the group all thought it famous, Bertram suggesting that they go snowballing.

"You cannot have thought, Bertram," said Mrs Allen in a quiet voice. "It will be impossible now for us all to get home."

"Oh Lord, yes. What's to be done?"

Everyone was by this time assembled in the drawing room and Prudence rang the bell for the housekeeper.

"Well, this is unexpected, to be sure, but I'm sure we will manage. It seems our party is to be extended beyond this afternoon. I beg you will all remain here, for it is evidently unwise to travel in this weather."

Mr Godwin, looking out of the window, turned back to face the room and said, "You are all consideration, Miss Fairham, but we are very close by and I believe, if we have the carriage called immediately, we might safely venture out."

"And Mrs Lambert and I are your nearest neighbours. I feel sure Mr Godwin is right and we would be loath to put you to so much trouble. Please forgive us. It has been a most enjoyable day, but I think we must take our leave of you, and with no little haste."

Prudence went into the hall and despatched the footman to order the conveyances to be brought to the front of the house. Turning to the housekeeper, who had appeared from below stairs, she said, "Mrs Wakefield, I fear I must rely on your ingenuity to accommodate some of our guests. Eight will be leaving, but I believe the rest will remain. Do what you can, please. I feel sure that the military gentlemen will have no objection to sharing a room and, of course, Mr Bertram and Master Francis."

Returning to the drawing room, Pru found that Becky had prevailed upon the squire and his family to remain. There was no question either that the Colbornes would return home, upon confirmation of which Bertram exclaimed, "Famous! We can play snowballs after all!"

Prudence was undaunted by the prospect of entertaining so large a group of people for what might be several days. She was pragmatic as well as capable and set her mind to pondering what plans could be made to amuse such a varied number of individuals. With the departure of the Godwins and the Lamberts, Bertram had lost no time in pursuing his ambition to lark about in the snow and had taken with him the younger members, Maria and Louisa Allen, on the advice of their mama, pausing only to avail themselves of some outdoor clothing before joining in with enthusiasm. Prudence looked out the window in time to see Bertram stuffing a snowball down his brother's neck and subsequently manfully placing himself between a missile and Maria Allen and thus being struck on the forehead. She smiled, satisfied that entertaining young people who had, most of them, so recently left the schoolroom would not prove to be difficult. Harder it would be, she thought, to find a sufficiently varied programme for the rest, but here she had reckoned without the ingenuity of her visitors.

"Ah, Miss Fairham, we have not been idle in your absence," said Mrs Allen. "Captain Staveley and Mr Bannerman have devised so many activities for our amusement that I dare say we might be entertained for nigh on a month without one of us becoming bored."

Prudence, though willing enough, sincerely hoped it wouldn't be necessary for such a length of time. Becky looked at her, her eyes brimful of laughter, but it was Hester who said, "I am astounded at the inventiveness of these two gentlemen. You will be left with nothing to do, Pru, for they have taken it all in hand."

"Then I am grateful to them indeed," she replied with a smile that matched her aunt's. "What, pray, do you have in store for us, or dare I not ask?" She turned to the two who, heads together, were compiling a list, having availed themselves of pen and paper. Jack replied with such a warm look that she was, for the moment, a little taken aback, but as he continued she put it down to her imagination.

"You will recall I once told you that my time in the army was not all fighting and that we might on occasion spend many an hour playing cards. There are several games to choose from but in addition there is charades which, in your absence from the room, found approval from all. And Bannerman here suggested Cup and Ball and Paper Ships."

"Rhymes with Roses is another and will show us if we have any budding poets in our midst," said Hugo. "And spillikins is always popular."

"If we are to play spillikins, I must insist that Becky be banned from the game. Having recently seen how steady her hand is, I doubt there is anyone could beat her. Such an unfair

118

advantage cannot be allowed," Pru said with a laugh. "It would seem you have left me with only the task of consulting with Cook to ensure we are suitably fed during your stay. I could not be more delighted."

The snow stopped falling during the night but left behind a thick layer on the ground the next morning. Prudence and Jack went to the stables before breakfast and spent some time, mostly in companionable silence, grooming their respective horses. Pru laughed as Firefly nudged forcefully with her nose, demanding her usual piece of apple.

"She needs no words to convey her wishes to me, for I could be in no doubt as to what she is after."

"Storm is the same," said Jack. "If I make any attempt to brush his flanks before giving him a treat, he turns his head and shuffles his feet, and he will not stand still until satisfied."

There was silence as they continued with the task in hand, but after a while Pru leaned her elbows on the wall that separated the two stalls, a rueful expression on her face. Jack looked up and smiled, the same warm smile she had seen the previous day, and she experienced a feeling of pleasure that they were once again on good terms.

"And what exactly is that supposed to mean?" he asked.

"What is what supposed to mean?"

"What a bouncer! Tell me, is something bothering you?"

There was something, it was true, and she voiced her concern that some of those who were now confined to Daventry House might wish to be elsewhere. "I was so careful to arrange yesterday's luncheon at a time when my guests might have ample opportunity to reach home before dark. And now some are stuck here, probably for several days, and there is nothing I can do about it."

Jack grinned back at her over the wall. "I am convinced you have nothing to fear in that regard. All you need do is provide sustenance and leave the rest to me and Bannerman. Between us we will keep everyone entertained."

"And I cannot tell you how grateful I am. And here are Fitz and Oliver come to help, and I am sure they too will enter into the spirit of the thing."

Most of the guests had arrived in carriages and several grooms were attending to their employers' horses, but Fitz and Oliver were keen to do the work themselves. The stables were extensive and had been refurbished to an excellent standard, built in such a way that the wind did not come whistling through during inclement weather. After spending an hour or so there, all four walked back to the house together to find that the younger members of the party had already breakfasted and were well on the way to building a very fine-looking snowman.

CHAPTER THIRTEEN

Thanks to the efforts and enthusiasm of Staveley and Bannerman, there was not one member of the party who felt a desire to be elsewhere. With William frequently falling into a comfortable doze beside a roaring fire, Becky and his wife were learning more about each other and the different lives they had led. Hester professed herself to be unsurprised by her in-laws' treatment of their daughter, having known both before their demise.

"I came to believe that they were more concerned about the opinions of their friends and neighbours than the happiness of their own children. To me they were always polite, but there was a coldness of which I can find no trace either in you or your brother."

"No, and had you known Sally you would have found her to be the same. As children we were, all of us, allowed into the presence of our parents for only half an hour each day. You will not be surprised to learn therefore that we grew up with little love for them and found our affection in each other instead."

"I always wished for a sister. Though Hugo and I are fond of each other, the number of years that lie between us mean we have little in common. It would, I believe, have been different had he been a girl, or I a man."

"Well, I for one am delighted you are not a man, Hester. You have become like another sister to me."

"In that regard we are both content, I think. And through you I may learn of all the places I have longed to see. Bertram and Francis came along so soon after our marriage that

William and I have had little opportunity to travel, for to take them with us was impractical and I would not have left my children for such an extended period."

Life had been hard for the young Mr and Mrs Standish, something Hester gleaned more from what Becky left unsaid than what she revealed. But it had been romantic in all senses of the word and the young couple, even after they were wed, had never shown any inclination to return to England. "Although now that I no longer have Monty at my side, I am happy enough to be home," Becky said.

"And I am so glad you are here. Men are all well and good, but there are times when one needs a person of one's own sex to confide in. I don't know how it is, Becky, but close as William and I are, there are times when what I say seems to go completely over his head."

Squire and Mrs Allen were happy to preside over the younger members of the party, usually accompanied by Hugo Bannerman, who it seemed never tired of entering into their childish games with as much enthusiasm as any of his juniors. In the afternoons the whole party would gather in the drawing room and, of all the activities organised for their entertainment, charades proved to be the most successful, even the squire foregoing his dignity to join in. After four days it was with a certain regret that everyone acknowledged that the snow was beginning to melt nicely and it was time for the party to break up. In one regard Prudence was not sorry. Hugo Bannerman had intensified his pursuit of her to such a degree that in the privacy of her bedchamber Becky had remarked on his perseverance.

"It would seem his intentions are serious after all," she remarked. "This is no longer the mild flirtation you told me of. Would you be happy if he made you an offer?"

"Indeed I should not, and that is the one reason I am glad the weather is clearing. In all other regards I have enjoyed these few days immensely. Of late, though, Mr Bannerman has become too particular in his attentions for my liking and I shall be glad to see him gone. While he has been our guest it has been impossible to snub him, and I fear he may have read more into my hospitality that I intended."

"Do you dislike him, then?"

"Not at all, but neither have I developed any degree of attachment that would make me wish to marry him. In any case, why are we talking thus? He has made me no offer and I sincerely hope he leaves without doing so."

"I too, if those are your sentiments. There is no doubt, however, that he has been a great help in keeping the rest entertained, particularly Louisa Allen. He did much to put her at her ease. Such a shy little thing, and with Bertram having eyes only for her sister and Francis not yet being in the petticoat line, I believe she would otherwise have retired into her shell."

Pru's wish was not to be granted, for on the day of the Colborne family's departure Hugo had succeeded in finding her alone, having waited patiently for her to return from her morning visit to the stables.

"Miss Fairham, I cannot remember when I have spent a happier few days and I must thank you again for inviting me."

"Not at all, Mr Bannerman. It has been my pleasure and indeed I don't know how we should have managed without your help, for your ingenuity in finding diverting occupations for the younger members of the party was second to none. It did not escape my notice either that you were instrumental in helping Miss Allen overcome her bashfulness."

"Well, I am sure I had as much enjoyment as any. I had forgotten how amusing childhood games could be. But, Miss Fairham, you must allow me to say that my greatest joy was in having the opportunity to spend so much time in your company. Forgive me, I would not have spoken so soon, but I must return to London shortly and know not when I shall be back in Somerset."

It was evident that Mr Bannerman was about to declare himself, and Prudence did what she could to prevent it. "Naturally we will all be sorry to see you go, but I do hope we can meet again the next time you visit your sister and brother-in-law."

"As to that, you know well enough what is my situation. To my shame I have used William abominably, but I cannot be sorry because it led to my meeting you. You cannot be in any doubt as to my feelings. I have no fortune to offer you. Only my hand and a heart that has been yours almost since the first moment I saw you."

He moved towards her but she held up her hand. "I am fully conscious of the honour you do me, sir, but I long ago decided that the married state is not for me. Please say no more and allow me to continue to call you a friend."

Hugo looked crestfallen but countered immediately, "I shall not despair. Had it not been necessary for me to remove myself from the district, I would have kept my own counsel. Give me leave, I pray, to call upon you again when I return. In the meantime I shall endeavour to put my affairs into some sort of order in the hope that my suit will be more acceptable to you."

"It isn't that. If I returned your affections…" She left the rest unsaid and he bowed over her hand, kissing her fingers lightly before stepping away.

"I will return as soon as I may and I sincerely hope I will persuade you to change your mind. I thank you again for making these weeks the happiest I have ever known."

He left the room immediately and there was no sign of discomfort when he took formal leave of Prudence and Becky in the courtyard an hour later. His manner was as usual, but for Pru the incident was the only thing that cast a shadow over the last few days. She hoped fervently that when he picked up his old life he would forget all about her.

Captain Staveley too had observed the growing advances of Hugo Bannerman and, while Prudence revealed no indication as to her feelings for the man, it seemed to him that she was enjoying the flirtation. While she gave him no overt encouragement, she as surely did not give any suggestion that his attention was unwelcome. Jack became aware of a jealousy so intense it took him by surprise. All at once he was brought to acknowledge that this woman whom he had known so well for so long was more to him than just the daughter of a dear friend. Love had crept up on him unsought and it caught him off guard. Unschooled in the art of dalliance, he had no way of interpreting the exchanges he had seen between Prudence and Hugo. What he did know very well was that she treated him, Jack, like a brother, just as she had always done. Thus, in one respect, he too was glad when the house party came to an end and he no longer had to watch and wonder.

CHAPTER FOURTEEN

Jack had organised a treasure hunt which was to begin early one morning a fortnight later and would culminate in a feast in the dining room at the manor. He and his fellow soldiers had spent two wonderful days riding the estate in search of places to secrete the prizes, but it was Bunting who was the most ingenious for he was the most knowledgeable, and it was he who formulated the clues. In each place was hidden a tankard, a crop, a pair of riding gloves or some other such bounty.

In addition to those residing at Fairham, the party was to be made up of William Colborne and his sons, it being considered a lucky coincidence that they were to be home from university that same weekend. Squire Allen and his elder daughter, Miss Maria Allen, were also to come, together with Mr and Mrs Lambert and their daughter, Fanny, the younger Mr Lambert being up at Oxford. Prudence was to make up the last of the group, Becky having declined the invitation, forming the intention instead of driving over to spend the day with Hester and the girls.

The day dawned bright and sunny. That it was cold deterred no-one, for they would soon warm up enough after a quick canter. Bunting had been clever with his clues, giving no advantage to Pru who knew the land as well as he did, but it was she who discovered the treasure hidden in the old oak. "Though what I am to do with a pair of men's riding gloves I am at a loss to know," she said, laughing when all were back at the manor and enjoying a fine repast.

"You must allow me to purchase another pair for you, in blue to match your habit," Jack insisted.

"No, for that would be most unfair to the rest who did not uncover any of the hiding places. I shall, if you have no objection, give them instead to my Uncle William."

Colborne turned from his conversation with the squire to say, "What's that? Did I hear my name?"

"You did indeed, sir," said Jack. "Miss Fairham wishes to make you a gift of the gloves she discovered in the oak tree."

"Delightful. One can never have too many pairs of gloves. Thank you, my dear."

Jack took them from Prudence and handed them to their new owner, but as he did so his fingers brushed hers and he sighed inwardly, wishing he could take them and raise them to his lips.

Jack and Prudence saw little of each other in the next few weeks, though they met occasionally at other people's homes. On the Fairham Manor Estate work had begun in earnest and, thanks to the plans having been drawn up in such detail, once the foundations were in place the buildings seemed to emerge with unexpected speed. Staveley hoped that his grandfather would have approved of what was being done with such a large part of the money he had bequeathed to him, for there was no holding back when it came to providing everything possible to facilitate the rehabilitation of the men for whom it was intended.

The days flew by and, with the help of Olly, Fitz, and Bunting, what had started as a dream became a reality. Others labouring on the site were astonished at the involvement of the gentry folk, but what they did not take into account was that these were ex-soldiers to whom idleness was alien and who were not afraid to get their hands dirty. Simpkins, too, spent many hours overseeing the project. As spring approached, Jack consigned to his two friends the task of posting north to where their old regiment was stationed to meet with the commanding officer. He would like to have gone himself but, as he said regretfully to his friends, "The building work is at a stage where, should a mistake be made, it would be costly and time-consuming to rectify. I wish I could come with you, but I fear it is out of the question."

Fitz and Hervey were charged with finding suitable candidates to fill the places available. Sadly there were fewer vacancies than there were those to fill them, particularly as Jack had decided only to bring ten to begin with. There was room for a greater number but, with no experience, he wanted to ensure that they knew what they were doing sufficiently well before asking the wounded to commit themselves. Fitz and Hervey, having gleaned what information they could at the barracks, thereafter travelled the country, seeking to interview the chosen few, for it was by no means certain they would all wish to come.

Simpkins was to engage the services of a local doctor, willing to deal with men who had suffered both physically and mentally and close enough to visit daily, should it be required. Nurses would be on hand as well, but it was the unseen wounds that would require the most care. The men would need to be taught occupations that would make them feel useful again; that would make them feel proud, rather than ashamed, of what they'd become.

Jack passed a most pleasant day at Daventry House, having ridden over to enlist Pru's help regarding the entertainment of the prospective inmates. "I would like to have some form of activity ready to engage the men when they are not learning a skill or receiving rehabilitation in some other way."

"Come and join me in the drawing room, and we will discuss what might be suitable. Becky has not long driven over to Wexford Hall, so we shall not be disturbed," Pru said, pausing to ring the bell for some refreshment. "Do sit down, Jack, and tell me what you have in mind."

He chose rather to stand, pacing up and down in a restless manner, throwing ideas at her, asking for her opinion.

"I will not say another word until you are seated," she said laughingly, "for I cannot concentrate while you stride about the room. Ah, here is the tea. Do be still for a while and let me think."

He sat while she poured the tea, trying to look contrite and failing entirely.

"There is much I would like to discuss with you, but tell me first what plans you have to give these boys some useful employment. For young men who have been used to such an active life, and these more than most, it must be intolerable to be forced into stillness, or to walk only haltingly with the aid of a crutch. Even you, able-bodied as you are, seem to be finding it impossible to sit still."

She was right, and he jumped up again as if to illustrate the point, helping himself to another cup of tea. "Between us, Simpkins, I and the rest have come up with several ideas which we hope will suit every situation. For some, confined to a chair but with the use of their hands, we are dedicating one entire room to learning woodcraft." Jack continued with his theme, speaking of simple pieces of furniture or even the possibility of developing a skill in carving. "And for those who prefer an outdoor life, there are countless jobs that need daily attending to in the stables. There is always the tack to be polished, and the making of saddles and bridles are, I am sure, occupations that can be carried out from a seated position."

"These are good suggestions, I agree, but what of those men who have lost not a leg but an arm? Have you any ideas for them?"

Jack told Prudence that they had discussed this situation and found it potentially harder to resolve.

"We used to have a one-armed gardener at Fairham who helped George Jenkins. There were several jobs he was able to do. Or," Pru added thoughtfully, "there are always things in the house that require polishing. Not a skilled activity, I grant you, but a necessary one nonetheless. But we are not speaking of officers here, I presume, but of men who were in the ranks."

"You are right. It is to be hoped that my fellow officers will have family and resources to aid them which the ordinary soldier will not. We cannot help everyone, and it is my considered opinion that we should direct our efforts at those men."

"Then we have only to discuss what recreational activities we might put in place during the hours they will not be working."

"Exactly, Pru, and that is why I have come to enlist your aid."

It being a beautiful spring day, they decided to stroll around the garden while they discussed this aspect of the project. Prudence asked if Jack had thought of installing a billiard table. "It is a skill those in wheelchairs could participate in if they have both arms."

"I knew I did right to come to you. I'm partial to a game or two myself, but it is something I had not yet thought of in this regard."

Card games were an obvious option, for even with only one hand a man might manage by laying them in front of himself on the table and picking them up one by one. Even spillikins was not out of the question. Charades found favour with both of them because it was something everyone seemed to enjoy and was a way for the men to engage with each other rather than the solitary occupation of reading, which might lead to isolation if it were the only choice.

Prudence walked with Jack to the stable. When Storm was saddled up and ready, he took her hand and, unable to resist, kissed her fingertips before mounting and riding off. She watched as he rode away and was surprised to find she had enjoyed the experience.

CHAPTER FIFTEEN

Becky was humming to herself as she drove to Wexford Hall, for it was an occupation which much suited her. Indeed, she had earned a reputation as a notable whip and it had given Monty Standish no small pleasure equipping his wife with the finest turnout. The phaeton she was driving was not of the high-perch type, a much sportier and altogether more daring form of transport, and one of which she had considerable experience. However, she had, for once, erred on the side of caution, judging it to be unsuitable for her current circumstances. There was nothing sluggish about the horses Jack had recommended she purchase to complete the equipage. They were a beautiful pair of matched bays — a little challenging, perhaps, to an inexperienced driver but she held them together without difficulty. They were quite fresh to begin with and covered the ground with ease. After a while she slowed them to a trot, giving herself time to look at the surrounding countryside. How familiar it was, even after so many years. Yes, it was good to be home. Good too that her brother had not inherited their parents' strait-laced morality.

Susan and Sophie, who must have been on the lookout for her, were waving from the front step as she drew to a halt in front of them. Sophie stood in silent admiration while Susan said, "Oh my word, Aunt Becky, aren't you just the thing? I am so envious!"

"They are beautiful, aren't they? And so well-behaved. I can take you for a turn later if you like. You too, Sophie."

The footman had run to the stables to fetch a groom to accommodate the horses and, upon his arrival, all three went inside. After allowing the girls to spend some time with their aunt while taking refreshment, Hester banished them to the schoolroom so she could enjoy a comfortable chat with Becky.

"It seems an age since I have seen you. You are well and truly settled at Daventry House now?"

"We are, and it suits us admirably. Prudence and I live in complete harmony, coming together when we wish, which I must tell you is often, or engaging in individual pursuits. You didn't know Sally, I am aware, but Pru is as like her mother as can be, both in looks and in temperament. I feel more that I have gained a sister than a niece. And, my dear, to have discovered in my brother's wife such a charming woman…" She paused and for a moment a cloud distorted her features, but she recovered soon enough. "I had not thought when I returned to England to find such contentment. In fact, I feared greatly that I would once again be rejected, so you may imagine my delight in you all."

"Forgive me, Becky, I have not previously asked for I did not wish to distress you, but this past year must have been most difficult for you. William and I have talked about you, I hope you do not mind. We are happy you have found accommodation so close by, and now that the weather is improving it is to be hoped that you will join us often when we are engaging with our neighbours. There are many who would be delighted to meet you."

Becky was under no illusion as to her sister-in-law's motives. She and William would see her marry again and would spare no pains to put suitable candidates in her way. They were happy and wished those around them to be happy too. Becky, though, was not yet ready to relinquish her widowhood. She was far more concerned about Prudence, and said so.

"I too would hope to see her comfortably established," Hester replied. "She seems content enough with her single state but it will not do, not forever."

"True, but she is an independent spirit, and my understanding is that she has rejected every opportunity that has come her way, preferring her own company rather than being tied to a man she could not love and respect. She is, after all, a Colborne, or from that stock at least. Though I dare swear you are able in the nicest way to bend William to your will, we are not any of us easily persuaded."

Hester knew it to be true. "I had hoped when we were confined at Daventry House during the snow that she and Hugo might make a match of it. I have never seen him so enchanted by a woman before. Not that there's anything to say to that, for we don't see much of him. But he is to visit us again next week, and that is in itself unusual. Unless his pockets are again to let, I must wonder if he comes to see Prudence."

Becky was at a loss as to how to respond. She could hardly tell Hester that she and Prudence had discussed her brother's attention and that it had been unwelcome. Instead she merely commented that they had seemed to strike up a great friendship and no doubt Prudence would be happy to see him again. There was a gentle tap on the door and their confidences were at an end.

"I am sorry to intrude, Mama, but Aunt Becky did say she would take me and Sophie for a drive before going home and we were wondering if she might have forgotten."

"Not at all," Becky said. "It will soon be time to take my leave, so perhaps you might have my phaeton brought to the front of the house and we will do just that."

Becky went to indulge her nieces before returning home to warn Pru of the imminent arrival of Hugo Bannerman.

"Aunt Becky, dearest Aunty Becky, I fear you will be sorely displeased with me, for did I not promise to look at these samples while you were out?" said Prudence, the wicked gleam in her eyes giving the lie to the mournful tone in her voice. "And you are anxious, I know, to order the chair covers without delay."

"Oh no, Prudence. You promised!" Becky replied, with such a straight face that for one moment Pru thought she was indeed upset. But her aunt couldn't maintain the deceit for more than a moment, and the corners of her mouth once more turned up. "Tell me what was so important that you must needs leave such a pressing task."

"I have had such an exciting time. Jack Staveley has been here. He arrived not long after you left, and we spent a long time discussing the project at Fairham. I am so pleased to be involved, for it is such a worthwhile thing to do. He came to ask my advice."

"Well, that's very flattering, to be sure. Were you able to help?"

"I was indeed. He was particularly concerned as to how to entertain the men during their recreational hours. The rest I believe he, Simpkins, Fitz and Oliver have well in hand. How we talked. It was quite like old times, when my father was still alive." She paused as emotions that she kept so well in check thrust themselves forward, causing her to feel a large constriction in her throat. Becky, understanding, waited for her to continue. "He had already thought of all the obvious things, but he was particularly delighted with my suggestion of installing a billiard table. And then we took a walk in the gardens and he is not long gone, so you see, don't you, why I have neglected the samples."

If Becky thought Pru rather more animated than usual she forbore to mention it. It wasn't for her to upset the apple cart and, if Prudence and Jack were once again on good terms, so much the better. "Well," she said, "I am delighted you have had such an exhilarating day, but I fear I must warn you your peace is at an end."

Pru looked up at her, curiosity writ large upon her face.

Becky, removing her bonnet, sat down before continuing, enjoying the increase in anticipation. "I am reliably informed that Hugo Bannerman returns to Somerset next week, for who should know his movements better than his sister?"

At that Pru laughed and exclaimed, "If even half the things Mr Bannerman told me are true, his sister would be the very last person to be taken into his confidence. On the other hand, if he is to stay at Wexford Hall I suppose it is necessary she should know in advance."

"She seemed absolutely certain of the fact and even told me she hoped for an alliance between the two of you."

"Oh dear," Pru remarked, biting her lip. "I do hope I didn't give Hester the impression that I was on the catch for a husband. I did not tell you at the time, for it seemed an unkind thing to do, but Hugo did indeed make me an offer before he left the county. Naturally I refused, but he told me of his intention to return when he had put his affairs in order. I can only assume, if he is back so soon, that it is to renew his proposal, for he assured me such was his intention. I had hoped that once he returned to town his thoughts would have taken a different direction. Tell me, Becky, what shall I do?"

"Well, my dear, nothing would make me happier than to see you established, but if Mr Bannerman is not the man for you it will be necessary for you to be more firm in your rejection. But we could be wrong, of course. He may merely be returning to visit his family and you are worrying for nothing."

"Perhaps," Pru replied, but she didn't believe it. Something other than affection for his sister was calling him back.

And so it proved to be. Scarcely a week later Pru looked out of the drawing room window to see a rider approaching the house. Not Jack, she knew, for she would as readily recognise Storm as Firefly, and her fears were found to be justified when the horse came close enough for her to see it was Hugo Bannerman on his back. She clicked her tongue, which attracted the attention of Becky.

"What is it, my dear?"

"'Tis only that your sister-in-law's brother pays the promised visit. Oh dear, I sound churlish, do I not? Perhaps he just comes to pay his respects. I beg you, Becky, not to leave us alone."

Becky was surprised. It wasn't like her niece to hide from a difficult situation. She nevertheless gave her promise. Both ladies rose and greeted their guest as he was shown into the room. His manner was easy as ever, and at first he made no attempt to separate Pru from her aunt.

"My dear Mrs Standish, Miss Fairham, I could not come into Somerset without as soon as possible making a call to thank you once again for your hospitality when I was last here. I come bearing an invitation from my sister, who begs you to join us for dinner on Friday. Bertram and Francis are returned home as the Lent term has finished and my sister has a mind to hold a family get-together."

"Do sit down, Mr Bannerman. Permit me to ring for some refreshment," Becky said, and did so. "Tell your sister that I shall be delighted to see my nephews once again and I'm sure I may speak for Miss Fairham when I say that she will visit with her cousins, is that not so, Prudence?"

"Of course. For one who has been the only child of a single parent all my life, the excitement of having an extended family is far from having worn off."

Conversation flowed easily, Hugo enquiring as to the progress of the ladies' refurbishments. Becky was placing his teacup on the small side table when he turned to Prudence and said, "I remember when I was last here that you had extensive plans for the gardens, which I could not see on account of the snow. Perhaps you would join me out there now and point out the changes you wish to make."

"What a splendid idea," Becky interrupted. "Do let us all go," she continued, thus fulfilling her promise to Prudence, whose gratitude was expressed upon his departure even before Hugo was out of sight, both of them waving him off.

"Have I told you that you are my favourite aunt, dearest Becky? It may seem immodest of me, but I fear we have only postponed the inevitable. I cannot like the way he looks so warmly at me."

"I believe you are right. It might perhaps be kinder to let him have his say, for at least then he would know where he stands."

Prudence for once did not confide in Becky. She had, for a while, been considering an alliance with Hugo Bannerman, should he renew his offer, and it was for this reason she had avoided being alone with him. He was a personable man, always neatly but not ostentatiously attired. In company too he was charming and able to join in whatever entertainments were offered, be they childish or otherwise. His love of riding was another point which in her eyes made him a suitable candidate. Only something was missing. It was not a thing Pru could put into words. She had consequently chosen to give herself more time.

Bah, she thought. *How conceited I sound. I am by no means certain he wishes any longer to pursue me.* She gave herself a mental shake. *You are too nice in your tastes, Miss Fairham.* But it wasn't that, she knew. If she married, she wanted it to be for love, and nothing was more certain than that she didn't love Hugo Bannerman.

CHAPTER SIXTEEN

"I know the work isn't finished, but we could no more leave these two behind than turn our backs on the enemy." Standing on the front steps of the manor, Fitz was explaining to Jack and Bunting why they had hired a coach to bring Morgan and Hewitt, two ex-soldiers, back to Fairham. "You wouldn't believe the circumstances in which both were living. Morgan's stump is causing him near unbearable pain, and he had no doctor attending him. We found him in abject squalor at the mercy of anyone who chose to taunt his altered state. Do people not know what these men did for their country?"

"I take it Hewitt is in no better case if you have brought him too."

"No, dreadful. His wounds are perhaps the more difficult to cope with because they are all but invisible. He has the use of his limbs and his sight is unimpaired, but he suffers constantly as a result of shrapnel injuries and has a tendency to lash out at the slightest provocation, or even none at all. He will be the harder to help, I fear."

Fitz was angrier than Jack had ever seen him and suggested that he delay the rest of his tale until the men were settled. "The accommodation is all but finished in the rehabilitation centre, but I would suggest you bring them into the house for the time being. And send for Doctor Ellis to come in the morning. They can remain here until he or we judge it time to move them. That's right, Hervey," Jack said, turning to his friend as, with Bunting's help, they aided first one and then the other soldier from the carriage and into the house. "Mrs Jenkins will know what to do. I shall suggest she puts them up on the ground floor. It will be easier to take them outside when the weather is kind. Bunting, please find her and see what you can arrange between you."

Morgan had been helped to a chair in the hall, but Hewitt was pacing up and down. It seemed impossible for him to be still. Jack turned his attention to them.

"That will do, soldier. Be seated if you will."

Hewitt recognised the voice of authority when he heard it and subsided at once into a nearby chair. The captain was grateful that he had responded so readily, having had doubts as to the outcome. Perhaps the man just needed to be given some direction or, at the very least, something to focus on other than himself. It remained to be seen.

"Welcome to Fairham Manor. Lieutenants Fitzroy and Hervey will have explained much to you already of what we hope will happen here. You have served your country well and we are proud of you, but the war is over now and your personal circumstances have changed. We will do everything we can to make you comfortable, but this will be no easy ride. When you are recovered from your journey, we will discuss what occupation will suit your future." He smiled briefly. "One thing I can promise you. You will not be idle. I never knew a soldier yet who could be still for five minutes. What you need, gentlemen, is something to do. Ah, here is Mrs Jenkins. She and Bunting will help you to your rooms and we will meet again later for dinner. I dare swear you are both hungry."

Hewitt followed Mrs Jenkins with a stiff gait but unaided. Bunting had conjured up a wheelchair and followed with Morgan.

"Right," said Jack, turning to Fitz and Hervey, "come into the library and tell me all about it."

An hour later Captain Staveley was in possession of some very gruesome facts. It hadn't been difficult to find men who might prosper at Fairham. Harder had been deciding which to leave behind.

"Well, we said that we would confine ourselves in the beginning. If things go as we hope, then we have the space to expand. Yes, I know," Jack said, raising his hand as Fitz moved to speak. "While we wait, there are other poor wretches living in hopeless misery. That said, until we have felt our way and know what we are doing, I wouldn't exchange one miserable state for another, something we could easily do if we allow our enthusiasm to carry us away."

"You were always a good campaigner," Olly remarked. "With the resources you have put in place, I make no doubt we will see speedy progress, but I agree. It would be easy to make a mistake, and we are dealing with men's lives here."

Dinner was a quiet and somewhat awkward affair. Fitz and Hervey, having run themselves into the ground over the past few weeks, were on the one hand feeling the anti-climax and on the other keen to get on with the job. Both Hewitt and Morgan had become introspective since returning from the battlefield, a means of self-defence that the rest perfectly understood but something which was difficult to deal with. In the end it was Jack who took the underlying tension out of the situation. He hadn't been a leader of men without learning how to handle most circumstances.

"The doctor will be here tomorrow morning to assess your needs and give us an indication of what he hopes you may be able to achieve in the future. As you know, the purpose of you coming to Fairham is to find for each of you an occupation suited to your abilities in order that you may move on with your lives." He paused for a moment, putting his elbows on the table and steepling his fingers. "I know that doesn't seem possible at the moment, but I can assure you we will do everything we can to ease your passage. We have, all of us, watched our brothers in arms make the ultimate sacrifice, but in a way your own losses are even harder to bear. Never underestimate what you have done for your country, for assuredly we do not. As soldiers you have been accustomed to being busy. You will be busy again. For tonight, though, you may retire as soon as you wish. Get what sleep you can and we shall begin in the morning. But, before you go, Lieutenant Fitzroy, Lieutenant Hervey and I would like to raise a toast in honour of you both and all who, like you, were ready to give their lives for what they cherished most. Because of you we are able to look forward to a time of peace that has been lacking for so long. Our women can rest easy in their beds knowing their menfolk are home and safe. So, gentlemen, I give you 'The Regiment'."

It stirred them as he had hoped it would. They retired shortly afterwards, followed soon by Fitz and Hervey. Jack, watching the embers die away in the fire, thought of Major Fairham and hoped he would approve.

Doctor Ellis came in good time the next day and examined the men, afterwards going to the library to discuss his findings with Jack.

"Morgan and Hewitt are both suffering a significant degree of pain. I have drugs which can help them and, though I fear it will never leave them, it will be managed to a level at which they will be able to function effectively rather than, as they are doing at present, focusing on their injuries and all that they signify. They have had far too much time to reflect on what, if even half of what they've described is true, have been the most shocking circumstances."

"From the little that Fitzroy and Hervey have described to me, they have been suffering a living hell."

"That these men who thought only of their country should have been abandoned in this way! It doesn't bear thinking about. Except, Captain Staveley, you have thought about it. So I will tell you straight. What they need is occupation. Most of their problems lie not in their physical disabilities but in their mental state. They are soldiers, accustomed to being commanded. Well, it's up to you to lead them. In the meantime I have left some medication with Bunting, whom I trust to administer it according to my instructions. I shall return in two days to see how they are going along and if I need to adjust the dosage. I wish you luck, Captain Staveley, and I honour you for what you are trying to do here. Remember, the most important thing is to keep them occupied."

Jack, with the aid of Bunting, took the two soldiers to the rehabilitation centre. It was necessary to take them in the gig, as it was too distant either to wheel Morgan or for Hewitt to walk and neither was able to ride. It was during the short journey that Jack saw the pain etched on their faces and realised what an ordeal just getting to Fairham must have been for them. Neither complained, though each winced involuntarily when the gig jolted them. On arrival they were taken to the accommodation block, where Fitz and Hervey were found in discussion with Simpkins. Each room was fitted out simply but in a way that a man might put his own stamp on it.

"Ah, gentlemen, it is a pleasure to meet you," the agent said. "I hope you approve of what we have done. I fear it will be necessary for you to remain over at the manor for a few days as we are not quite ready for you here, but you can in the meantime familiarise yourselves with the layout. When you have done so, we shall move on to the other buildings so you can see where the work will be done. There are several opportunities and we must find what suits your abilities, for you look to be the sort of men who will perform any task as best you are able."

Even this short inspection and the discussion of what was to come produced a significant change in the soldiers. While their reactions were quiet, it could be seen that Morgan sat straight in his chair and Hewitt, who had been advised by the doctor to use a stick to aid his walking, moved with a greater degree of determination. They were to be given something to do, and this alone was reason enough to hope.

Jack was pleased with what he saw as a positive result and, with Fitz's permission, he took his mount and rode over to the stables, where he saddled up Storm. The sooner Morgan and Hewitt were put to work the better, but just as important was the need for them to enjoy their recreation. He trotted at a leisurely pace to Daventry House, whistling as he went. Prudence would be as anxious as he for the men to make progress, and he judged that a woman's touch was just what was needed to encourage them.

They would be able to pass the evenings well enough, with cards, billiards and a drink or two. There was no question of rank or status here. On the battlefield all had mixed together and so it would be at Fairham. Less easy would be filling the daylight hours, for it was not to be expected that in their reduced physical state they could work the day through. And that was, Jack anticipated, where Prudence would come in. It was his hope that she might return with him that morning to meet Morgan and Hewitt and even perhaps to make a start. He was therefore more than a little dismayed when shown into the drawing room to find Hugo Bannerman was there before him.

"Jack, how delightful to see you," Pru said, jumping up and holding out her hand in greeting. "No need to introduce you to Hugo, of course."

Quite unjustly Jack was disturbed by the use of the other man's first name. What was the fellow doing here again anyway? But he knew only too well that he could attribute his feelings to jealousy. Bannerman was affable and likeable and those days they had spent together at Daventry House, confined as they were by the snow, were hugely entertaining. He swallowed his irritation and moved to meet him.

"None at all. I remember him clearly as the man I marked out never again to challenge to a game of spillikins. You warned us at your house party only of Becky's skill, so I was not on my guard. No more shall I throw down the gauntlet." Jack was smiling, outwardly in greeting and inwardly at his wish that they lived in a time when the glove could indeed have been flung in defence of a lady. But Pru wasn't his lady to defend, and he could never forget his ineptitude the day he offered marriage. Etched even deeper was her anger. He had no chance with her, he knew that now. It had taken many months for them to revert to their former ease. His mistake would always lie as a barrier between them, deeply hidden but ready to jump to the surface at a wrong word. He would not give that word, but it was hard to see Prudence the object of another's gallantry. "And speaking of Becky, how is Mrs Standish?"

"Well, I thank you, and visiting at Wexford Hall."

"I was fortunate," Hugo added, "to pass her on my way here, and she reined in to exchange pleasantries with me. She obviously takes as much pleasure in her equipage as Miss

Fairham does when riding Firefly. But you must excuse me, for I stopped only to pay my respects on my way to visit a friend who lives in Wells. I hope you will allow me to call again upon my return in a few days."

"Becky and I are always pleased to receive our friends. Do wait here, Jack, while I show Hugo to the door."

In the few moments he was waiting, Jack reflected that sometimes events were a matter of luck. He had gone from being cast down by Bannerman's presence to the hope that Pru would, after all, be eager to accompany him.

"He is a delightful man but has taken to visiting rather frequently since returning to Somerset," Prudence said as she walked back into the drawing room. "I cannot be quite comfortable when Becky is not here. You know how little I regard convention, but it would not be well considered if people knew I was receiving a gentleman alone."

"Is that my cue to leave?" Jack asked with a laugh.

"Good heavens, no. You and I have been friends forever. It is quite different."

Jack didn't know whether to be pleased or dismayed. It was evident that in Pru's mind Bannerman might be regarded as a suitor and he not.

"Now, tell me if you will how things are progressing at Fairham."

"That is the very reason you see me here today. Fitz and Oliver returned yesterday and brought with them two men whom they felt it impossible to leave behind. They are sleeping at the manor until we decide who will stay with them at the rehabilitation centre, for we would not like to leave them alone. The doctor has been to see them and they are even now inspecting the premises."

"But that's wonderful! When may I meet them?"

"Would now be convenient? I was hoping you might return with me. Let me advise you of what the doctor said and you will understand why. He is happy with all that we have put in place, or are planning to, but it will not be possible or practical for the men to work every waking hour. It's my thinking that they will benefit, forgive me, from seeing a woman every now and then. As soldiers their time will have been spent exclusively with their fellows, but we would like there to be as much normality in their lives as possible. I had thought we might alleviate their endeavours from time to time by reading to them, and I believe this will be better received from you than from me or Fitz or Oliver. What do you think?"

"I think we have talked for long enough. Just give me time to change into my habit and I will ride over with you. Shall I meet you out front?"

"Storm and I will be waiting for you."

She did not keep him above ten minutes and they went along in companionable silence, each enjoying the pleasure of riding. Prudence had paused only to choose two books from the library and place them in her saddle bag. They went directly to the rehabilitation centre to find that the rest had already left, but instead of pursuing them they waited long enough for Pru to see what had been done since she'd last visited.

"Oh, but this is wonderful! So much good will be done here." She turned to Jack and clutched his arm. Her voice was filled with emotion as she said, "My father would have been so proud. His men were always of paramount importance to him, as they are to you. Come, let me meet Morgan and Hewitt."

They rode on to the manor, but all Jack was aware of was the burning sensation where Prudence had touched his arm.

CHAPTER SEVENTEEN

Prudence was surprised to find how disturbed she was by the men's condition, but she was a soldier's daughter and knew how to hide her feelings. They were not to know that the unconscious gesture of tweaking one of her curls was a sign of anxiety. She had, after all, waved her father off to war many times and had long since learned to conceal her distress by biting the inside of her lip, even at times drawing blood. She didn't do so on this occasion, but her tender heart went out to them as she was introduced to Morgan and then Hewitt. Though some of the horrors of battle had been recounted to her in the past, for she'd always begged Angus to tell her something of what he had been through, she learned that there was a distinct difference between the telling and the seeing.

Neither man was aware of her apprehension, however, as she said, "How happy I am to see you both here. I hope you don't think I shall be fussing, for I expect that would irk you terribly, but I would count it a privilege to spend some time with you. Perhaps, when you are feeling more settled, you might like to talk to me of some of your comrades, for I can tell you that when my father came home on furlough he could speak of nothing else." She paused, hoping she had not overstepped the mark, but neither appeared put out or turned his head away so she continued with a smile. "I must tell you that you do us all a good service by coming to Fairham. Since the captain and Lieutenants Fitzroy and Hervey sold out, they have missed the Regiment and all it entailed. Well, naturally we cannot duplicate that, but it is to be hoped that we will form our own small community here. And don't think you will be idle, for I know that Captain Staveley has great plans for your future."

This time there was a discernible reaction, a stiffening, and she responded immediately.

"I can see that you fear what is to come. That you may not even have dared to look ahead. Allow me to say that, though you will have a home here for as long as you may wish, you will become adept in some useful occupation and will once again be able to make your own way in the world. You may not think it at present, but I promise you it will be so. You knew my father, the major. Rest assured, my word is as good as his."

Pru was gratified to see that both men seemed more relaxed and Jack, who had been holding his breath, let it out slowly but silently. Soldiers were used to straight talking. They had to be, but these two had suffered much so it was good to see that they seemed willing once more to rise to the challenge. Bringing books turned out not to be such a good idea. It was difficult to engage either Morgan or Hewitt and it became evident very quickly that, though trying to be polite, they were not in the least interested. Jack, who preferred to read in silence rather than listen to others, was entirely in sympathy with them. He had noticed at the rehabilitation centre how their attention had been arrested by the sight of the billiard table, already installed in one of the recreation rooms.

"Perhaps you would care for a game of billiards," he suggested. "There is a room here devoted to nothing else and I have spent many pleasant hours there."

"I doubt my ability to reach the table, Captain, or to play with any particular skill from the confines of my chair," Dafydd Morgan declared, obviously with regret and perhaps a tinge of bitterness also.

"But you will not know unless you try, and we are not challenging you to a tournament. What do you say, man? Shall we give it a go?"

"If you put it like that, sir, how can I refuse? I just hope I don't tear the baize in the attempt."

"Between you and me, Dafydd, I must confess there is something I once did myself which necessitated having it recovered. What about you, Nathaniel? Will you join us?" Jack asked, turning to the other soldier.

"Aye, Captain, I'm happy to try."

They all adjourned to the billiard room, Pru included, and while Fitz and Hervey good-naturedly propped up the wall, each with a drink in hand, Jack positioned Morgan's chair near the table. He took some moments to adjust his position before using a rest to support the cue, but when he took aim he missed the ball altogether. His frustration was evident, but Jack put a hand on his now rigid shoulders and laughed.

"I see your style somewhat resembles my own. Come, try again. It cannot be expected that you will get it right first time."

This time Morgan managed to tip the ball. It didn't move far but it was a start, and he was keen to try once more. As his ability improved with each attempt, so did his temper. For the first time in as long as he could remember, Dafydd Morgan was enjoying himself.

"Your turn now, Nate," he said, offering the cue to Hewitt. "You can do no worse, that's for sure." Hewitt was certainly more successful, but the pain he suffered was etched on his face. Pru looked at him with a deal of concern but judged it unwise to comment. Fitz pushed himself off the wall and went to put an arm on Hewitt's shoulder, asking quietly if he had taken the medicament supplied by the doctor.

"I don't believe in all that namby-pamby stuff. What do you take me for, a weak woman? Begging your pardon, Miss Fairham."

"I take you for a soldier," Fitz replied in a much firmer voice, "and therefore one who is used to taking orders. If you choose to remain here, that is what you will do."

There was tension in the room, for all could see the struggle Hewitt was having with himself. Yes, he was in the habit of obeying orders, but a man had his pride. Grin and abide it, he had always been taught. He looked from one to another, five faces all showing sympathy, and was mortified that tears sprang to his eyes. He dashed them away in anger, but it was Prudence who spoke.

"You have shown enormous courage in coming here, Nathaniel, such courage as great as any you may have displayed on the battlefield. You owe nothing to anyone in this room. Rather it is we who are beholden to you. I would ask you therefore to allow us to help you. You haven't even been at Fairham for one day yet. Your rehabilitation will take many weeks. Months, even. Please allow us to facilitate it if we can. I for one would deem it an honour."

Nate's shoulders sagged and he stumbled to a chair, putting his head in his hands and weeping silently. Pru went and knelt beside him, placing one hand on his knee.

"Don't be ashamed of your tears, Nathaniel. You have earned them. We will try again tomorrow, and as many tomorrows as it takes. Now I believe I must return to Daventry House before the light fails, but I shall see you again in the morning, never fear. Captain Staveley," she said, turning to Jack, "perhaps you will escort me home so that you may be back in time to dine with these brave men."

"Allow me to walk you to the stables. I suspect Bunting will have been watching the time and had the foresight to have the horses saddled and ready."

"Good afternoon, gentlemen. I shall see you on the morrow."

Prudence and Jack were silent for the first part of their journey, allowing the horses to stretch their legs into a canter. As they reined in to a walk, she turned to him and said, "Must I ask your forgiveness? I fear I may have gone beyond what is acceptable to you."

"What on earth are you talking about, Pru?"

"When I was talking to Nathaniel Hewitt. You may remember that I said he may remain at Fairham as long as is necessary. It was not my place to speak on your behalf."

"What nonsense you do utter sometimes," Jack replied, smiling back at her but aware of the necessity to answer truly but without causing her offence. "We have discussed this project so many times, it is as much yours as mine. Just as, even though you no longer reside here, Fairham will always be a part of you." He leaned across to touch her hand where it rested lightly on the pommel, and once again she was acutely aware of his touch. He continued almost without pause. "Dafydd and Nate have a tough time ahead, just as those other boys will when they join us later. It is necessary that we treat them firmly, but this must also be tempered with kindness. You bring something that the rest of us do not have, and it is as critical to their rehabilitation as any exercise or training will be. You refer, I imagine, to Nate breaking down, but is that a bad thing, do you think? We can only guess what torment he has suffered alone because he is a man and men don't cry. I am strongly of the opinion that it will only have done good. A hurdle that needed to be overcome before he can move forward."

"In that case, I shall return tomorrow as promised. My groom will accompany me, for your time will certainly be better spent here with the men."

If Jack was disappointed at having to forego a ride with Prudence, he refrained from saying so. It made good sense and in the end she came not mounted on Firefly but driven by Becky, who had expressed a determination to meet the newcomers. She had lived on the Continent for many years and was familiar with army types, having encountered them on several occasions when their duties permitted. Morgan and Hewitt very soon responded to her easy manner.

Doctor Ellis had returned a day earlier than intended, bringing not only the promised medication but also several pages of written and illustrated instructions. "Having examined both yesterday," he told Jack, "I was able to form a better idea of their needs. See if you can persuade them to complete these exercises at least once a day, preferably twice. You will notice they are different for each man. Do you know how long it will be before the rest arrive?"

"Not too long now, for the work is almost complete and we feel organised and confident enough to go ahead, particularly if you will provide the same service."

"Naturally I shall do so. Call me if you need, otherwise I shall return in a week to see how they go on."

He had put both men through their designated exercises so it was judged time, when he left, to give them some respite. Becky suggested she might drive them around to give them a larger view of their surroundings, and Prudence went along to point out each landmark and to prevent her aunt getting lost, being as she was unfamiliar with the estate. The officers, left to their own devices, went straight to the rehabilitation centre to see what they might do there. Bunting, who had aided both men into the carriage, wheeled Morgan's chair to his workshop which was situated adjacent to the stables. By dint of attaching a handle to each of the wheels he rendered it possible for the user to manoeuvre himself, rather than always having to rely on someone else to push him. It was only a temporary solution until a more modern device could be ordered, but it would most assuredly help for the time being.

If Dafydd Morgan and Nathaniel Hewitt wondered why Captain Staveley and not Miss Fairham resided on the estate which bore her name they knew better than to ask but, as they drove around, it was evident from those they met that she was highly regarded by them all. If there was an underlying reason behind Pru's choice of places to visit she did not make it obvious, but it could be seen that, for instance, Morgan's interest was aroused at the smithy's workshop. Not only were horseshoes being made but brasses and other accoutrements were also being fashioned there. The blacksmith was working on some as Becky drew the carriage to a halt. He rose immediately to greet them, but not before the soldiers had been able to see that he'd been seated.

"Good day, Miss Fairham. Aye, but it warms my heart to see you here."

"It is kind of you to say so, Jacob, and of course I could not pass this way without visiting you. Is Mary well?" she asked.

"That she is. Hold fast and I'll fetch her, for it's certain I would have to go without my dinner if I let you leave before she had a chance to pay her respects."

He returned minutes later with his wife, carrying ample refreshment for the travellers. While they drank, Morgan engaged him in conversation and when they left Prudence was satisfied a seed had been planted. She was surprised to find, when later they visited a small hamlet and encountered the local parson, that the connection between him and Hewitt was almost tangible. Pru wouldn't have taken Nate for a religious man but, using the stick as the doctor had suggested, he walked a way along the road with the parson, totally absorbed in their conversation. This was a possibility that had not occurred to her, but as an occupation it could well suit this serious young man. What with visiting farms and stopping at a leather worker who was fashioning boots, she began to feel hopeful that there might be several opportunities for future employment. All the while Becky had maintained a cheerful flow of conversation and, though both men were quite evidently exhausted by the time they returned to the manor, each was lighter of spirit, something which prompted Jack later to say to Prudence that he had known all along her inclusion in the project would be invaluable.

"Your gratitude must go also to Becky, who kept them entertained with such anecdotes as I would never have been able to supply." She looked serious for a moment and he raised an eyebrow in question. "You will grow weary of me saying so, I am sure, but Papa would have been so proud of what is being done here. That you do it in his name is an honour and I commend you for it. And I thank you."

She could not have known how Jack longed to sweep her up in his arms. Instead, all he could do was make light of his contribution and say that thanks must go also to his maternal grandfather, whose funding had made the whole thing possible.

CHAPTER EIGHTEEN

One morning a few days later, just as Prudence was preparing to leave home on one of her now daily trips to Fairham, she was delayed by the arrival of Hugo Bannerman, on his way back to Wexford Hall after visiting his friend in Wells. They met in the hall and he observed that she was dressed for riding. He said with all his usual enthusiasm, "I see you are about to go out. Perhaps you will permit to accompany you. I'm sure my horse would not deny me a good gallop."

"You mistake. I am not on this occasion riding for pleasure but am on my way to Fairham Manor."

"Then allow me to escort you."

Though she would have preferred to go alone, Pru could think of no reasonable excuse to refuse him. As they slowed to a trot, Hugo told her of his few days visiting with his friend. It had been pleasant enough, he said, but confessed he'd been dipping rather too deeply and was once again constrained to return to his sister's home, probably for considerably longer than he might have wished. He related the tale as a joke, but she could not like this side of him and found his remarks about his sister and brother-in-law offensive. But then she had never in her life taken advantage of anyone's good nature as he appeared to be doing. Unconsciously she stiffened and her leg touched Firefly's side, causing her momentarily to break into a canter. She brought her horse back into a slower pace and turned the subject, but could not rid herself of a sense of discomfort.

Hugo had assumed Prudence was making a neighbourly call and was surprised to learn how involved she had become in the work that was taking place at her former home. Unaware of the circumstances that had caused her to leave and Captain Staveley to be in residence, he could have no idea how much her feelings were torn, visiting daily her erstwhile home. Even in this short time she knew her interaction with the wounded soldiers was proving effective, and more would be arriving very soon. She felt invigorated, as if she had for the first time found a purpose in life. But that purpose caused her pain every day when she had to leave behind what had once been hers. Valiantly she had tried to conceal these feelings from Jack. There was no way she would allow Bannerman to have even an inkling of how she felt, so she spoke only of the good work that was being done.

"Is there any way in which I could be of assistance?" he asked as they turned into the gates of the Fairham Manor estate.

"It isn't for me to say. It is Captain Staveley who is in charge, and it is he whom you must ask."

She was surprised when he did just that, for she had thought once they arrived at Fairham that he would ride on to Wexford Hall. Instead he accompanied her inside. Jack, who was coming out of the library as they entered the hall, pulled up short, surprised and more than a little displeased when he saw Bannerman, his hand on Pru's elbow as they moved forward to greet him.

"I hope you don't me dropping in like this, Staveley. I was escorting Miss Fairham and she has been telling me of the good work you're doing here. I wondered if perhaps there was any way in which I might aid these poor creatures."

Perhaps he didn't intend to sound condescending, but both Jack and Prudence bridled. However, Jack wasn't going to turn down any help he could get and volunteered to take Hugo to the rehabilitation centre where the men were now residing. He turned to Pru and said, "I wonder if you might go first to the stables. Bunting asked me to tell you there is something he wishes to discuss with you."

"Yes, of course. Firefly has already been taken there but I can easily walk across. Shall I see you later at the centre?"

"Certainly. And Fitz and Hervey too, I hope. As you know, they have thrown themselves like demons at this project and are even now escorting four others who will join us today. If all goes to plan they can see the doctor, who is due to visit the day after tomorrow. If need be I will send for him sooner. But Bannerman and I will come with you first to the stables, for I need Storm to take me over there. Will your horse be fresh enough, Hugo, or shall I have another saddled for you?"

"It is only a short distance from here to Wexford Hall. I am sure he will be up to it if given a short break before I leave."

Leaving Prudence with Bunting, the two men rode on together.

"Good day, miss. I cannot say how it warms my heart to see you here every day. It's where you belong."

Bunting had known Pru all her life, and he knew that what he said might cause her some distress, but the words were out before he could stop them. It seemed such a natural thing.

"We all know how my circumstances have changed, Bunting, but I must say that the work we are doing here is so all-consuming that I feel it would be the same even if it were taking place elsewhere."

"You always were a busy one. You were never meant to lead a life of ease and indolence."

She laughed and asked why he had wanted to see her. It was about Morgan, he said. Had she observed his interest when visiting the smithy? He had confided in Bunting that he would be willing to try his hand at aught that might have anything to do with horses and that he would be honoured if he could play a part in their welfare. Since Bunting had adjusted his wheelchair, it had given him a degree of independence he hadn't known since losing his leg. "Though there is no doubt he is in considerable pain, Dafydd Morgan would haunt the stables if permitted to do so. You would not believe how eager he is when he comes here. He has no fear at all, and somehow the horses seem to sense how he respects and loves them. Not one, even the most spirited, has kicked out at him and I can tell you he has wheeled that chair of his pretty close to them. He had even been seen attempting the use of crutches, and it's my belief it's on account of getting even closer if he can."

"That's such good news."

"Indeed it is, Miss Pru, and I wondered if you might perhaps drive him to the smithy, for he cannot take himself, so that he may observe and learn. Jacob is willing, I know, for I have asked him, and Mary will keep any eye on him so you need not remain but just return when it is time to bring him back."

"I had not thought we would be so fortunate so quickly. Does young Hewitt express any interest in anything that you have seen?"

"It's harder for him, I think, even though he retains all his limbs. It is my belief the medication barely touches his pain. All the more reason to find an occupation which absorbs him, for there is little else to take his mind away from his bodily ills."

"Are you out of your mind? Whatever were you thinking?"

Prudence could hear Jack's voice though she was still some distance away, having just arrived at the centre. She thought she had never heard him sound so angry and held back, not wanting to intrude on an argument that didn't concern her. She was surprised to hear that it was Hugo who replied.

"You are right of course, Staveley. I had hoped to distract the men with a game of cards. It didn't occur to me that I was doing wrong, but I can see that perhaps…"

He left the sentence unfinished and Jack said, "I would ask you to leave now, Bannerman. These men's futures are hanging by a thread. I would prefer you not to become involved."

"I beg your pardon. I shall go immediately."

As Prudence approached, Hugo swept passed her, barely acknowledging her presence, his face flushed with a fury as evident as Jack's had been. She continued on to find him pacing up and down like a caged animal.

"What is it, Jack? What has he done? I'm sorry, I could not help overhearing."

"Would you believe it? That man came here professing a wish to help. I don't know any soldier who doesn't pull out a deck for recreation so, when Bannerman suggested it, naturally I acceded, grateful that he was trying to help. I left the room and came back later to find them playing for stakes which they had no resources to fund and a pile of promissory notes in front of Bannerman. You know what soldiers are like, Pru. Their pride would not let them admit they could not pay. I swept the notes off the table and tore them up in front of him."

"Bravo. What a crass thing to have done. I credited him with more sense."

"And I," said Jack, calming a little now he had given vent to his spleen.

"Where are they now, the men?"

"Probably still sitting at the card table. I must go to them. Will you join me?"

Prudence smiled but said she thought perhaps it would be inappropriate and she'd find something else to occupy her while he dealt with the problem. They met up a while later and he explained that they had been as much shocked by his own behaviour as anything else but were grateful to him for digging them out of a hole.

"Evidently Bannerman made it nigh on impossible for them to refuse and then he raised the stakes. What could they do? They have nothing but their pride."

"And more than a small percentage of that." She fell quiet for a few moments and it didn't take much imagination to guess what she was thinking. Had her father not also been a compulsive gambler?

"Prudence, I didn't mean…"

She held up a hand to prevent him continuing. The pain was writ clearly upon her face and he waited for her to compose herself. "I will never understand what it is that drives men like my father and Bannerman to hazard in this way. It's like a fever in the blood. I betray no confidence, for he is entirely open about it, when I tell you that Hugo comes into the country only when he is purse-pinched."

"Perhaps of late there has been another reason," Jack said, regretting the words even as he uttered them.

"I have no knowledge of his motives," Pru replied, prevaricating, for this was not a conversation she wished to have.

He allowed the subject to drop and asked what Bunting had wanted to see her about. This was much safer ground, and Pru told him of her resolve to drive Morgan to Jacob's smithy if it could be fitted in with his schedule.

"The only schedule is to do what is best for the men. Aside from anything the doctor has dictated, it is up to us to find the best way forward for each individual. Prudence, when first I mooted this idea it seemed even to me to be crazy, but now it has taken on a life of its own. This is a campaign as important as any I have ever fought, and your aid is invaluable. You can provide things I never could, and if you told me now you wished to withdraw I would do everything in my power to persuade you otherwise." It was an impassioned speech and he grasped both her hands as he spoke. She returned his grip, for she felt as he did.

"It has become of paramount importance for me too. I feel now that I have an aim in my life which has never been there before. We are at one in this, Jack, and must work together to do what we can. You speak of campaigns, but this is one that will never end for there will always be those in need of help."

They moved apart again, he wishing their partnership could be something even greater and she with something stirring in her that she did not recognise.

Prudence and Becky saw little of each other these days, except to meet in the evenings. While Pru spent her days at the centre, Becky's friendship with Hester continued to flourish. They had accompanied each other on shopping trips to Wells and could often be found together, either at Daventry House or Wexford Hall. Her old home was a much nicer place now the atmosphere of bygone days was no longer there.

William was an easy-going man, welcoming his sister back into the fold and content that his wife should find pleasure in her company. Often out riding or taking his gun for some sport, he was unaware that calls from his neighbour, Benjamin Jarvis, had become more frequent. An old friend from Becky's youth, the pair lost no time in becoming reacquainted and Hester watched with satisfaction as the two reminisced together. Benjamin had a sense of humour as lively as Becky's, and it wasn't long before it became evident that their friendship was fast developing into something warmer. She would tell him of some of the outrageous things she had seen — and in which she had participated — while living abroad, and he delighted her with tales of former acquaintances.

Becky had made no particular mention of Mr Jarvis when they recounted their days' activities over supper so Prudence was more than a little surprised, when first she encountered him at a soirée which the Colbornes were holding, to observe the obvious affection each held for the other. There was nothing proprietorial in the way the gentleman behaved, but it was evident to anyone with a grain of understanding that he was deeply smitten. Her aunt too showed a preference which, though not overt, was recognised by the niece who by now knew her so well. The only thing that marred the evening for Pru was the presence of Hugo Bannerman and, though she could not be sure, it seemed that Hester and William were not quite as genial towards him as of late. She rather wondered if he had outstayed his welcome. Finding herself alone for the first time, she was less than pleased to see him approach. There was no avoiding him and he was as charming as ever but, in the light of recent occurrences, she would rather he had chosen someone else to speak to.

"Miss Fairham, it has become excessively warm in here. Perhaps you would care to take a turn about the terrace. Now that the evenings have become so mild it would, I think, be a welcome relief."

"I should be delighted," she said, with more politeness than truth. He took her arm and they went outside to where a few of the other guests had obviously had the same idea. Walking on, they entered the Spanish garden. Hidden now from view by its high walls, Hugo stopped abruptly and turned towards Pru, grasping both her hands. She tried to pull away but his grip was firm.

"Prudence, I can go no longer without telling you again how I feel about you. You fill my dreams. My waking thoughts are all of you. I have spoken to you honestly about my circumstances. I have nothing to offer you but my poor self."

"Please, Hugo, don't."

"It is useless. I have been hanging out for a rich wife and have instead found an angel. Marry me, Prudence, and I will spend my life trying to make you happy."

She started to protest and he released her hands, but only so he could wrap his arms about her. She began to struggle, unable to break free, but all at once relaxed and uttered breathlessly, "Oh, thank goodness." For one glorious moment Hugo thought she had succumbed, but he had not seen what she had. A hand fell heavily upon his shoulder and he was wrenched away. With one blow he was laid to the ground.

"You forget yourself, Bannerman," said the now hated voice of Jack Staveley. After that, Jack ignored him. To Prudence he said, "I fear it has become a little chilly. Allow me to take you back inside."

Jack explained that he had arrived late to the party and had walked in just as Pru and Bannerman were going onto the terrace. Waylaid by others who stopped to greet him, he followed the couple outside and, when he did not immediately see them, went in search.

"And thank heaven you did, Jack, for he was so carried away I had no means of holding him in check. To think I once thought he might make me a suitable husband!"

Jack was hardly surprised. Until he had shown his true colours, Bannerman had always appeared to be a personable and charming man. Remembering the party in the snow, Jack realised how he had himself been taken in. What affected him most, though, was that Pru should confide in him in this way. It saddened him to acknowledge that, had she regarded him as more than a friend, it was something she would have kept to herself. Concealing his own despair, he led her to a chair and went to fetch a drink to calm her nerves.

Prudence and Becky spoke only of inconsequential things on their way home from the soirée, for their groom could overhear everything that was said. Once inside the house, Becky said with a grin that she would retire to bed.

"Oh no you don't," Pru said firmly. "I want to talk to you. Join me in the drawing room, if you will."

Her aunt laughed and tripped ahead of her, having already anticipated that she was not to be let off lightly. She sat down and folded her hands demurely in her lap, but there was nothing demure about the way her mouth curled up at the corners. Pru wasted no time in confronting her.

"What a nice gentleman is Mr Jarvis. I believe him to be a childhood friend of yours."

"Yes, he is nice, isn't he?"

"He displays an air of mischief, wouldn't you say, Becky?"

"He has ever done so and led me many times into trouble in the past."

"Or the other way around, perhaps. Is there a Mrs Jarvis?" But she knew the answer already. It seemed that Benjamin's wife had passed away some three years earlier. Childless and with no other family, it had taken the combined efforts of his friends to lure him once more into society. Meeting Becky had, he had told her, brought him back to life. All this she related to her niece, eyes cast down, but Pru was not fooled.

"It was evident that this was not the first time you had met Mr Jarvis of late. Or even the second or the third. When I consider that you are in the habit of informing me of all your encounters with old friends, it seems strange," she continued in a conversational tone, "that you did not think to mention him to me."

Becky gave up all pretence and jumped to her feet, taking Pru's hands in hers. "Do you like him? Is he not an engaging companion?"

"He is indeed, and I am overjoyed to find you so animated. Have you reached an understanding?"

"Nothing has been said but I am hoping, I truly believe, that it will not be long before he declares himself."

"I could not be more pleased. I shall watch with interest to see how things develop."

Prudence was delighted but came quickly to the realisation that, should Becky and Benjamin make a match of it, it would be necessary for her to find a new home, for nothing was more certain than that her aunt would move out. There was no way Pru could maintain Daventry House alone, but the thought did not alarm her. She had grown considerably in the past year. She might, she thought, rent one of the cottages on the Fairham estate. The idea amused her. She was about to suggest that they retire when Becky said, "But what of you? I observed you going outside with Hugo Bannerman and returning with Jack Staveley, after which Hugo was no more to be seen. So tell me, what occurred?"

Pru grew serious once more and related what had happened. "It was awful, Becky. He had me held fast and I could not escape. If it hadn't been for Jack I don't know what would have happened."

"I am truly disappointed in that man."

"In Jack? Why, what has he done?"

"Don't be foolish, child. Bannerman has shown himself to be a man of easy charm with exceedingly good manners and an asset to any social occasion. It would seem there is another side to his character that he has kept well-hidden. I wonder what he will do next."

"I neither know nor care. It is a pity but I feel myself unable to visit the Colbornes while he remains at Wexford Hall."

"That is indeed a pity, but I perfectly understand. I shall keep you informed of the situation. It is to be hoped he will leave in the near future, particularly after what has occurred tonight. I think, now he has no hope of you, that he will find somewhere else to stay. Hester, I know, and almost certainly my brother, though he has not confided in me, have grown tired of their hospitality being so taken advantage of. Neither will be sorry to see the back of him and will not in future be quite so ready to welcome him into their home, I think."

"Then I shall say goodnight, Becky, and sleep well in the hope your future happiness is close to being secured."

CHAPTER NINETEEN

As the days lengthened the flow of visitors to Daventry House grew. Becky had renewed and enlarged her acquaintance. Many of these she had to entertain on her own, as Prudence spent increasing amounts of time at Fairham. The most prominent of her guests was Benjamin Jarvis, and there could be little doubt now that he was pursuing the widow with a view to proposing matrimony. With neither having any progeny of their own, there was no-one to consider but themselves. Vivacious as she had always been, there was now an added glow to Becky's demeanour. Often her friends would arrive only to be told that Mrs Standish was walking in the gardens with Mr Jarvis. They were in the rose garden one day when Benjamin plucked an early bloom and dropped to one knee in front of Becky, who was seated on a bench.

"My feelings will come as no surprise to you, Rebecca. These past few weeks have given me hope you might return my regard. I ask that you do me the honour of becoming my wife."

Becky laughed, a delightful sound, and drew him up to sit beside her. "Do get up, Benjamin," she said, accepting the proffered rose, "for we can talk far more comfortably this way." She put the rose to her lips and smiled coyly at him. "My answer is yes, of course. In fact, had you not asked me soon I make no doubt I should have given you a firm nudge, for it is my dearest wish to marry you."

It was a slightly dishevelled couple who returned to the house a while later. They had much to discuss. Becky had never visited his residence and he was concerned that she should like what would be her new home. Would she care to come, with Mrs Colborne perhaps, or Miss Fairham, to advise him of any changes she might wish to make before the wedding? Only a few guests at the ceremony, they decided, for while each was sociable in the extreme, both wanted their joining to be a private affair. He asked where she might like to go on their honeymoon.

"To my new home, if it pleases you, Benjamin. I have travelled enough for one lifetime. Although perhaps a trip to London would be nice, before it gets too hot to tolerate. Have I told you how much I like shopping?"

"You have not, but if you think to frighten me you are wide of the mark. I never knew a woman yet who didn't like shopping," he replied, his broad grin matching her own.

They would wait only until the banns had been read before marrying in the chapel at Wexford Hall, if Hester and William did not object.

Hester and William did not object, of course, and four weeks later Becky Standish became Mrs Rebecca Jarvis in a ceremony which was witnessed only by the Colbornes, Prudence Fairham, Jack Staveley and Squire and Mrs Allen. With no family of his own and Hester and William his closest friends, Benjamin was content to have it so. The couple left for the capital the following day, leaving a host of builders carrying out the desired work to Honeysuckle Cottage, a name which did little justice to the vast edifice which was to become Becky's new home. Before she left, she embraced Prudence and whispered in her ear, "You must remain at Daventry House for as long as you wish, just as we agreed. Do nothing in haste. We will speak more of this when I return to Somerset."

It was something they had discussed in the previous weeks. Both knew Pru would not remain indefinitely. With Hugo Bannerman long gone there was no longer any question of romance, but there was no lack of company. The army had been the focus of her life for so long that she found no difficulty spending her days with men who, even if no longer acting soldiers, were still of a kind with whom she felt most comfortable. The rehabilitation centre was full to its present capacity and, though there were plans to extend in the future, that must wait upon the success of the existing arrangements. It looked very much as though Hewitt's future would lie with the clergy, and it was to be hoped he would find some peace in that occupation. Dafydd Morgan was a changed man. It was no longer necessary for Prudence to drive him to the smithy as she had, early on, handed him the reins. His disability had proved to be no impediment to his driving skill and, now that he had become proficient with his crutches, he was able to get about independently.

Fitz and Hervey came and went at different times, visiting friends in various parts of the country but returning always to Fairham, for the work there had become a passion for them also. There was no shortage of social events as they had been welcomed into the larger community in the same way Jack had been. Invitations arrived as often for them as for him, and as their acquaintance enlarged they made the decision to purchase a property locally.

"We have taken advantage of your hospitality for too long," Fitz told Jack.

"What nonsense. I could not have achieved as much had you not been here. Mine is the debt."

"I believe, for all three of us, this has become a mission which gives us a new purpose in life, don't you agree, Olly?" he asked, turning to Hervey who was pouring claret into three glasses. "I shall never forget my time in the service of my country, but I wonder if you remember when we first came to Fairham and you talked about selling out and travelling the world. I knew then your heart wasn't in it."

Hervey laughed. "And no doubt I would have landed myself in trouble fairly quickly. One thing the army taught me is that I need discipline in my life. I'm with Fitz here, Jack. We have discussed this between ourselves and we'll find a nice place of our own nearby so as to be on hand to help you see this through. I'm afraid, Captain, you're stuck with us, like it or not."

There were no more protestations. Jack knew it would be far harder to run Fairham Manor Rehabilitation Centre — it now had a name — without the aid of his two old friends. Had they expressed a wish to leave, he would have done his level best to prevent them from doing so.

When Jack learned that Prudence had been seeking new accommodation, he was utterly exasperated.

"You are proud beyond reason," he said to her, his voice barely under control. "I know how stubborn you can be. Good heavens, woman, I served with your father for long enough. You must be aware how it chafes me that you will not take your rightful place at Fairham Manor but…"

"It is no longer my rightful place," she interrupted, her outrage as great as his own.

"…but, as you will not, would you perhaps oblige me by making use of the dower house? You are well aware that it has stood empty for any number of years and would benefit greatly from being occupied." He could see that Pru was about to interrupt again and put his hand up, while continuing to speak.

"It is not for me that I ask but for the men. You have expressed an eagerness to help and your contribution has proved to be invaluable. Consider, if you will, how much more convenient it would be if you were actually living on the estate."

Jack was not prevaricating and Prudence could not but admire his campaign strategy. Her temper subsided and she said, with no little humility, "Thank you. I accept."

He was astounded that she had succumbed so readily but what he had said made sense and, now that she was in the habit of coming to Fairham so regularly, the pain had become an ache and as such far easier for her to deal with.

"I am delighted, my dear," he said, taking her hand and kissing her fingertips. "Are you able to remain at Daventry House until such time as your new home is fit for habitation, which it most certainly isn't at present?"

"Becky and Benjamin have not yet returned from London and, even if they had, there is no urgency about my removal. It has been some time since I last visited the dower house, and even then it appeared thoroughly neglected," she said, wondering why her fingers should be tingling still from the touch of his lips. It was not the first time a man had kissed her hand, but it was not something she would normally expect from Jack. Unconsciously she rubbed one hand with the other and Jack, observing, thought she had found it distasteful and resolved to be more careful in future.

On Thursday of the week following Pru's decision to move to the dower house, Becky, having returned from her honeymoon, paid her a visit in their old home. Drawing off her gloves, she embraced her niece before standing back to look at her.

"You are looking radiant, my dear child. Work obviously suits you. I wasn't even sure I would find you at home."

"Indeed I am not often here. I never before had an occupation that so fulfilled me, other than riding. How indolent I must have been in the past. But what of you? And Mr Jarvis? Was the poor man required to hire an extra coach to bring home your purchases?"

"Not at all, for you will recall that you and I went shopping several times in Wells when we moved here to Daventry House. No, we visited the theatre."

"Ah, I envy you that."

"It was exhilarating, I must say. Also, we were invited to dine with members of Benjamin's club. He doesn't visit very often, but it was evident that they are long-standing friendships and keep in touch on a regular if infrequent basis. Their wives were delightful, all of them, and made us most welcome."

"You have not been idle, then."

"Not a bit. We drove in the park. In a hired vehicle, for we did not have our own in London, but we were stopped several times to pass the time of day by those who knew one or other of us. I was surprised to meet Lieutenant Fitzroy, who told me he had bolted to town for a few days and would pay us a courtesy call when we all returned to Somerset. A delightful young man. I am happy to see that he too has found a vocation."

"Yes, he is quite a favourite of mine. Now, do sit down," Prudence said, for they had by this time entered the drawing room, "and let us discuss what we are to do with Daventry House."

Becky pouted and said that surely Pru recalled they had agreed she could stay there for as long as she needed.

"I do and we did, but I have the need no longer. I am to take up residence at the dower house at Fairham." She looked around at the beautifully proportioned room, its furniture and hangings so exactly what she and Becky had wanted. "It is a pity to leave all that we have done here, but no doubt I shall have pleasure altering things there to suit my needs when I move." She laughed. "My one regret is that we never did hold the promised ball, and after all the effort we put into that apartment!"

Mrs Jarvis clapped her hands gleefully. "Why do you not hold one now, before you leave? I feel it would be a suitable way to mark the change in both our circumstances, don't you?"

"Oh my word, yes," Pru replied, as animated as her aunt. "Let me send for some tea, then we shall make a list of all those whom we wish to invite. And discuss the hiring of musicians, and what we would like to offer in the way of refreshment. In fact, perhaps our first list should be of all the lists we are required to make," she said, laughing.

Becky remained so long at Daventry House that she feared Benjamin would be growing anxious if she did not soon return to Honeysuckle Cottage.

"I shall come again tomorrow so that we may discuss this further. What time of day would be convenient so I may be sure of finding you at home?"

"The morning would be best, because that is when the men's time is given over to their various forms of exercise. For most it is an exhausting occupation and, left until later in the day, might prove too strenuous for some."

She went on to explain that it was of the utmost importance to return the ex-soldiers to the greatest level of fitness of which they were capable. While the ambition was to provide each with some form of training whereby they might in future support themselves, there would be little point in teaching them skills they were too weak to use. Most had arrived at Fairham in a pretty sorry state, having previously given in to the desperation of being a helpless burden. They were accustomed to helping others, not the other way around, and they did not easily accept assistance. Becky was shocked, but not surprised, to learn that more than one had expressed a wish to Jack that they had perished in the war, rather than lead the empty existence that appeared to be all that was left to them. One of those who had been chosen to come to Somerset had, Prudence told her sadly, put a period to his life a week before Fitz and Hervey had returned to collect him. "Such a waste, particularly after surviving the war. Sad too that there is a long list of men waiting for the opportunity to come, for we cannot care for them all. This man's place was filled immediately. I look forward to the time when we will be able to enlarge the facility to accommodate many more than we are at present able to do."

"You really have taken this to heart, haven't you?"

"I have, Becky. Those of us who were safe in England cannot imagine the horrors of war, but I for one did not anticipate that the horrors of their homecoming might be the greater."

Becky had pulled on her gloves now and embraced Prudence once more, beseeching her not to wear herself down to such a state that she might be unable to help. The ladies parted company, Becky to return to her husband and Pru to change into her habit so that she might ride over to Fairham. Yes, it would be much easier once she moved into the dower house.

"It may be that you will see less of me in the coming days," Prudence told Jack when she was leaving Fairham at the end of the day. "I must tell you that Becky came to visit me this morning and between us we have decided, before I move, to hold a ball at Daventry House, as was our intention when first we came."

Jack was in two minds as to how he should respond. Prudence owed him nothing, but he knew that routine played a major part in the rehabilitation of his men. On the other hand, if they were ever to become independent it was also important that they should be able to deal with change as it happened. In the end he realised that it was not the men who were his prime consideration but that he would himself miss Pru if she were to come less frequently. He berated himself for a selfish fellow and said, "I shall look eagerly for my invitation. Have you fixed on a date yet?"

"And what makes you think, Captain Staveley, that your name will appear on my guest list?" she said archly.

"If it does not I shall beg Mrs Jarvis to add me to hers, or I shall arrive and beg entry. Do you ask Fitz and Hervey also?"

"Of course. They are the most personable young men in the neighbourhood and no party would be complete without them." The smile that went with this remark was not lost on Jack and he declined to rise to the bait, instead changing the subject.

"Have you had any further thoughts about what alterations you might like to implement at the dower house?"

"I have indeed, and have engaged the services of the man who did such good work in setting up the centre here. He has drawn up some plans which I have inspected and hopes to begin work very shortly." She paused, her hand on Firefly's bridle, before continuing. "I am conscious of the service you do me by accommodating me in this way and I would like to say, for I haven't thus far, how grateful I am."

The smile left Jack's eyes and was replaced with a look so cold Prudence hardly recognised him. "I must inform you, Miss Fairham, that you are prone on occasion to speak utter balderdash. I think perhaps it's time for you to leave before I lose my temper, for I truly have no patience with your sentiments. You are aware how I feel about Fairham. Do you take pleasure in bringing this up again? You must surely know by now how much it rankles with me. Come, let me help you mount," he finished, and helped her up into the saddle, turning away even before she had given her horse leave to move on. She rode away, tears of rage whipped away by the wind as she spurred Firefly into a gallop.

By the time Prudence returned to Daventry House her anger had abated, but she was left feeling desolate. Jack was her closest friend in the world, and if he withdrew from her she would feel all the loneliness that had lurked in the background since her father's death. Finding her extended family had been a source of enormous comfort and she had a greater sense of belonging than ever before, but it was Captain Staveley who seemed to understand instantly when she made some remark with her features composed but all the while laughing inside. It had always been so. Only her father had shared the same appreciation of humour. Even Becky, outrageous and funny as she was, didn't quite reach that part of Pru known only to Jack. She dined alone and spent the rest of the time until she retired making notes ready for her meeting with her aunt the following day, but somehow the fun had gone out of it.

CHAPTER TWENTY

Lowness of spirits was not something Prudence could sustain for any great length of time, and when Becky arrived the next morning all her accustomed enthusiasm had returned. Her endeavours the previous evening had not been in vain. Her aunt found several sheets of paper on the table, each blank save for a designated heading to be elaborated upon, among them a guest list, refreshments, candles and decorations and entertainment.

"You have been remarkably busy since I last saw you," Becky said. "Shall we work together or independently?"

"I think it might be better if we made separate lists to be amalgamated when we have run out of ideas, don't you?"

"Yes, I agree, for when I talk about one thing another goes completely out of my head. Where shall we begin, do you think?"

They decided to start with the guest list. In the end the numbers were identical to their first previous dinner party, the one that had become a house party on account of the snow. In fact, the only difference was that Hugo Bannerman was thankfully no longer in the district and Benjamin Jarvis took his vacant space.

"Fortunately we may hopefully rely on the weather at this season," Becky said. "There is a full moon in three weeks. Are you free tomorrow to ride over to Honeysuckle Cottage if I am able, in the meantime, to procure some invitations? We may then write and distribute them all in the one day."

"Of course I will. Shall we turn our thoughts now to supper? Let us each once again take a sheet of paper and make our own list. It will be interesting to see how they differ. I think, though, that we should begin with white soup, do you not?"

"And I insist we have salmon pie. It is a favourite of mine. And quaking pudding." Becky jotted both down and added several others while Prudence did the same.

Some minutes later, Pru exclaimed, "All this talk of food has made me hungry. Shall I ring for a light luncheon? You can stay? Excellent." Both were satisfied with their morning's work and after their light repast took a walk together in the garden before Becky returned home, Prudence promising to join her the following morning.

She had intended to remain at Daventry House for the rest of the day, but her conscience piqued her. Tomorrow would be taken up entirely with writing and distributing invitations, and there would be no opportunity at all to visit Fairham. While aiding generally, she had also been working specifically with two men and being absent for two whole days would disturb the continuity she had been trying so hard to establish. There was still time, if she hurried, to ride over and spend some time with them. The morning had done much to restore her, but she was honest enough to own that she would have preferred the distance of more than one day before seeing Jack again. Berating herself for what she perceived as weakness, she mounted Firefly and rode the short distance to Fairham Manor.

"I had not looked to see you today," Jack said, walking out of the rehabilitation centre as Pru arrived. The words were welcoming enough, but the tone in which they were spoken most assuredly was not. She knew at once that she had not yet been forgiven, and again she felt anger and frustration well up inside. If either of them had reason to be resentful, surely it was she. She no longer blamed him for her father's weaknesses. Even while she remained saddened that her idol had had feet of clay, she remembered Angus with all the love of an adoring daughter. His passion for cards and the circumstances of his death only illustrated the exuberance of the man. Angus Fairham had been larger than life and he could have lived no other way, so he had chosen not to live at all. None of that was Jack Staveley's fault.

It seemed, however, that Jack had not forgotten yesterday's words, but what had she done, she argued with herself, other than try to make him understand that she was content with her lot? Except it wasn't true. Her motives weren't quite as pure as she would have wished. Somewhere deep inside, she knew of Jack's discomfort. Had she been kinder, she would have left the words unsaid. All this she acknowledged to herself, but it only caused her chagrin to increase and, instead of offering the apology she knew to be appropriate, she turned and left him standing while she entered the building. She didn't see him again that day.

Three days later, all the invitations had been written and delivered and the answers received. There was but one apology and that from Captain Staveley: *Unfortunately I have a previous engagement and will be unable to attend.* It seemed the rift between them was widening, as she could not believe he might be engaged elsewhere when all their local acquaintance would be at Daventry House. Had he been called away from Fairham Manor on some other matter she felt sure she would have heard, either from Fitz or Oliver, so closely was Jack tied to his project. With a heavy heart, she had to accept that their friendship would never be the same again. For a fleeting moment she wondered if she should withdraw from taking up residence at the dower house, but even in her own eyes it would be a sign of petulance.

A little more of the pleasure went out of the ongoing arrangements for the ball, but it would have been untrue to say she wasn't enjoying the experience immensely. Not for nothing had she acted as her father's hostess on so many previous occasions. Together with Becky, organisation went forward without a hitch. Musicians were engaged, her cook was given leave to employ as much help as she felt necessary, candles were ordered, decorations commissioned and after several changes of heart a menu was decided upon.

"Which leaves us with nothing more to do than return to Wells to have our ball gowns adjusted," Becky said.

The day of the ball drew near, and in the intervening weeks Prudence and Jack had done well to avoid each other as much as was practical. When they did meet, there was a forced politeness between them which even Fitz remarked upon when he and Hervey had both been present at a conversation about the men's welfare.

"It felt to me as though they were two business partners discussing the feasibility of a projected venture, rather than friends of many years' standing. What has happened, do you think, old boy?"

"I know not and I intend to keep well out of it. I would advise you to do the same."

"I agree. Shame, though. They've always got on so well before. I hope it doesn't mean Miss Fairham will discontinue her visits."

"No," said Hervey. "Icy cold as the atmosphere was, both are totally committed, of that there is no doubt."

"You're right, of course. As are we. Did you know Jack isn't going to the ball on Tuesday? I was never more astonished. He always loved a good party."

"I believe there's a lot more to this than meets the eye but, as we've said, it's best we stay out of it."

With hundreds of candles burning and their flames reflected in the numerous mirrors that graced the walls of the ballroom at Daventry House, there was no doubt that this was to be a glittering occasion. As carriage after carriage arrived and deposited its passengers, it became quite evident that the evening was to be a success. Prudence and Becky welcomed their guests together, the former insisting the party was as much her aunt's as her own. With everyone known to each other, there was no need for the formality of introductions.

Young Bertram was delighted to be able to renew his acquaintance with Maria Allen, having had little opportunity to see her since his last visit to Daventry House. He lost no time in soliciting her hand for the first dance and had to be reminded gently by his mother that it was impolite to spend the whole evening at her side and that perhaps he might engage with some of the other young ladies present. He was a trifle abashed, for in spite of his exuberance he was a thoughtful young man. However, before he left Maria's side he was fortunate to solicit a promise from her to take her into supper later in the evening.

In the yellow saloon card tables had been set for any who might wish to play. The squire was delighted to remove himself from the ballroom and settle down to a quiet game. He was joined by Benjamin Jarvis, who professed himself grateful to be seated for a while. "My good lady has given me so many tasks, I had forgotten just how arduous giving a party can be, pleasant though it is."

They were joined by William Colborne and Harry Lambert and spent the next hour enjoying their leisure before being summoned for supper, where they found many things to please them at a huge table. Pru and Becky had spared no pains to provide something for every taste and Fitz, who had escorted his hostess, proclaimed, "I am amazed the legs have not given way beneath their burden. If I may say so, your cook has done you proud, Miss Fairham."

"Oh no, Fitz, surely we are well enough acquainted by now for you to call me by my given name. Tell me, if you will, how are things at the centre? I have been so preoccupied here these past few days that I have been unable to visit."

If she had expected any news of Captain Staveley none was given. She had neither confirmation nor otherwise of his absence from Fairham. She was only told that there had been two new arrivals and that one in particular was giving them cause for concern. "He shows signs of aggression far greater than any we have seen so far. The poor man had his head crushed in and has lost the sight of one eye. Already he has displayed his rage in a physical manner so violent that it took three of us to restrain him. The doctor comes tomorrow and we are hoping something can be prescribed to calm the lad. He is but nineteen years old. It has been necessary to confine him to his room, so we are relying on something being done to ease the situation as soon as possible."

"Oh, poor young man," Pru said, her heart going out to this soldier whom she had not yet even met.

"Indeed, but we never, any of us, expected this to be easy. It is boys like this who most need our help."

"I will come tomorrow. Perhaps speaking to a woman might help him."

"I fear it would be too dangerous."

"As bad as that?"

"I am afraid so, Miss Fair— Prudence. Our hopes must rest with Doctor Ellis. I say, Oliver," he said, turning to his friend. "Have you tried the *oeufs au miroir*? And these syllabubs are the best I've ever tasted."

Talk moved away from Fairham and Pru left the two friends together to converse with her other guests. There were a few moments when she and Becky found themselves standing side by side, and they congratulated each other on the evening's success.

"I am so delighted we decided to go ahead, Pru. In fact, I think I will persuade Benjamin to hold a ball at Honeysuckle Cottage. The poor man will be horrified, but now that we have experienced it once it will be easy, I am sure, to replicate. Don't you just love having people around you, people who are so obviously enjoying themselves?"

Prudence concurred, but she couldn't help wondering what Jack Staveley was doing. Did he have people around him, or was he sitting alone at Fairham Manor? She gave herself a mental shake. It was none of her business, after all. Instead, she turned to Squire Allen and said, "You need not think, sir, that I will allow you to disappear once more into the card room. Not, at least, until you have danced with me as you promised you would."

He chuckled and confirmed that her suspicions were correct and that it had been his intention to do just that. "But I shall be delighted first to take the floor with you. What is it to be, Miss Fairham?"

"Why, the waltz, of course, Squire Allen."

"At my age?" he asked, aghast.

She let go of the laugh she had been holding in. "No, I would not be so cruel, but I would stand up with you for the cotillion, if you please."

"It will be my pleasure," he replied, politely if not entirely truthfully, for he had eaten his fill and would far rather have sat for a while. She knew it to be the case but she insisted, and he declared after that he hadn't enjoyed himself so much since he didn't know when.

Hester, who had been watching from the side of the room, told Prudence later that to begin with she had felt sorry for the poor man. "But it became evident very soon that he was embracing the dance with gusto. I expect the delicious punch helped as well. You are to be congratulated on your success, my dear. An excellent evening."

"Thank you, Hester. As much credit goes to your sister-in-law as to me, but I must say that I have enjoyed the whole, right from the moment when we first wrote out our guest list."

"I notice Captain Staveley is not here. Is he away from home? I do not hesitate to ask, for I know you are good friends and I feel sure you must have invited him."

Prudence took no offence but explained that it had been necessary, he had said, for him to decline, for reasons she was unaware of. What she didn't tell her aunt-in-law was that she was more than ever convinced his decision arose from the bad feeling that was now established between them. Pushing the thought aside, she checked once more to be certain that none of her guests was left standing or seated alone before taking a few moments to herself on the terrace. The weather had been kind and a full moon shone out of a clear sky. There would be no necessity for anyone to remain behind this night.

Mr and Mrs Jarvis were the last to leave, and the hug that Prudence and Becky shared continued for longer than usual.

"I fear this is the last time we shall be here together, Pru. You are moving next week, are you not?"

"That is the plan, yes. I cannot thank you enough for the time we spent together at Daventry House, Becky. But you are a married lady now, and I have a new mission in life. We will still be close neighbours, however, and I shall see you in two weeks at the Colbornes, will I not?"

"Of course, and I shall drive over to visit you often. Now that I have found you, my dearest niece, you may be sure I shall not let you go."

Benjamin Jarvis handed his wife into the carriage and, as she waved them goodbye, Pru took a deep breath and let out a long sigh. It was the end of another chapter in her life and a new era was about to begin.

CHAPTER TWENTY-ONE

A litter of puppies had been born in the stables since Pru was last at Fairham. She could hear them mewling as she settled Firefly into her stall and, after a short search, found them in the corner of an empty loose box, their mother curled protectively round them.

"Well, Tina, haven't you done well?" she said gently.

"Aye, but what am I going to do with six pups I don't rightly know," said Bunting, entering so quietly she hadn't even heard him arrive. "It will have to be drowning for them, I think, for it's unlikely I can find anyone to take 'em."

Prudence stood arms akimbo, her back to the young family, and stared defiantly at Bunting. "You will do no such thing. Why, you haven't even given them a chance. I would be happy to take one when I move into the dower house. A female, if there is one, and she will be company for me."

"I'm happy for you to have the pick of the litter, if that is your wish, but the rest must go."

"Oh, John, no! That would be too cruel. At least let me think about it before you take action."

She had ever been able to wind him round her little finger, particularly when using his given name, and he consented to wait a while. "But once they are weaned they must go, either to a new home or to the river."

With this she had to be content, but she determined it wouldn't come to that. Leaving the stables, she headed for the centre and visited each man in turn. Shortly after her arrival Doctor Ellis entered with Jack, who barely glanced in her direction. Hurt but determined not to show it, Pru said, "Good morning, gentlemen. I understand from Lieutenant Fitzroy that we have a new recruit. I would wish to meet him."

Jack had no choice but to acknowledge her. "I believe we must first hear what the doctor has to say. This man has problems we have not as yet encountered."

"Of course. I shall be in the recreation room when you have finished. Perhaps you might join me there."

She addressed neither man in particular and both sought her out after the examination. Doctor Ellis spoke first. "It is my professional opinion that it would be unwise for you to attempt any interaction with Skerrit for the time being, Miss Fairham. I have given him a sedative which I hope will help, but he is in a bad way and we must wait awhile to see if it is effective. In the meantime I must congratulate you on the change you have wrought here. There is no doubt in my mind that some of the success that has been achieved must be laid at your door."

Pru turned pink with pleasure and shot a quick glance at Staveley, but it seemed his attention was caught by something on the other side of the room.

"Now," continued Doctor Ellis, "if you will excuse me, I may as well check on the rest before I leave."

The two were left together, apparently without a word to say to each other. Pru was the first to gather her wits and, with an air as cool as Jack's, informed him that she was going to visit the dower house to see how things were progressing and would return later to aid with the activities that had been put in place for the soldiers. She turned on her heel before he had an opportunity to respond and left him wondering what on earth he might do to put this wrong to rights.

It was a fine day with a gentle breeze blowing, and by the time Prudence arrived at her destination she had succeeded in laying her dissatisfaction to rest. Not only that, but her excitement mounted as she examined everything that had been done. She was delighted. It was a smaller house than she was accustomed to but by no means too small for her comfort. Kitty would go with her, and Cook as well. The new housekeeper had also proved to be more than satisfactory at Daventry House and a footman and upstairs maid would complete the staff.

There were eight bedrooms on the two upper floors and, as she climbed the old oak staircase to the one she had chosen for her own use, Pru was delighted to look back down over the banister on the landing and see that all below was newly decorated and in readiness for her occupation. Her own chamber was almost identical to the one she had inhabited when residing with Becky, for she had chosen carefully then and had not yet tired of it. It would serve to make the move a little more familiar for her. The other upstairs rooms she knew also to have been completed but she didn't inspect them on this occasion.

Returning downstairs, the drawing room was her next destination and, content that her instructions had been carried out, she continued to explore the rest of the house. Standing once more in the spacious hall she twirled around, pleased with everything she had seen and eager to move in. There was only one shadow over her happiness and, as she could find no solution to improving the situation, she walked back to the centre, telling herself as she went that she had an important job to do. Anything else would have to be dealt with as best she could. Four days later she moved into the dower house.

The new residents were making good progress, only Skerrit proving to be difficult to handle. Nor had they yet found any occupation that appealed to him. He was sullen and aggressive, and a huge amount of time and patience was required by those in charge of his care. It was considered too dangerous for Prudence to engage with him and, though this saddened her, she could appreciate why. Never before had it so chafed her to be a woman and thus unable to be involved.

Spring was well-advanced and Pru had taken to carrying her chosen puppy with her to the centre. Still only six weeks old, Dash and her siblings were not quite ready to leave their mother permanently, but it was her new owner's plan that she should not come to her entirely unknown. The idea turned out to be beneficial for reasons she had not anticipated, as it could be seen that everyone's mood lifted immediately when she appeared, some of the men asking if they could pet the little dog. Prudence approached Jack with the suggestion that the rest of the puppies take up residence at the centre when they were ready to leave the stables. During these several weeks their relationship had not improved, their exchanges being merely civil.

"An excellent idea, if you can find someone to take overall charge of them," he said, allowing a little warmth to creep into his words.

"There will be more than enough volunteers, I am sure. Whether or not we should allow the men to adopt their own is questionable, I think. For a start, there are not enough to go round. However, given time we may see some of them bonding and the decision will be made for us. If you are happy with the prospect, I shall inform John that there is no longer any need for him to drown the puppies."

It was, of course, well past the time when it would have been a feasible option. Bunting had known from the start that Pru would find a solution, just not that it would be so close to home.

Fitz had been away for some weeks, visiting his parents, but had now returned. "How have things been during my absence from Fairham?" he asked when he, Oliver Hervey, Prudence and Jack were sitting down for a meal to discuss future plans.

"Most are doing well, though there is little if any change in Skerrit. I just pray that in time things will improve for him," Jack said, frustration and sympathy both making themselves felt. He sat back, nursing a glass in his hands, and looked from one to the other. "I have been wondering if you think we are experienced enough now to expand. Prudence has, I know, chosen to make the centre her mission in life, but what of you two? It has been some months now. I am aware that you have made your home in the county and that you have received many invitations from our neighbours, though it puzzles me to understand why, such a pair of reprobates as you are." He laughed and then became serious again. "But what of your work here? Do you see yourselves continuing or, now that we are established, would you choose to move on?"

"I thought we had made ourselves clear, Jack. I know I speak for Fitz as well when I tell you that I can think of nothing more rewarding than to help these poor blighters who have given so much."

"I had hoped that would be your decision. What do you say, then? Shall I go ahead with plans for expansion?"

All were in agreement and wanted to press on with as much speed as possible. Though none of the current places had yet been vacated, they all felt that Dafydd Morgan would not long remain. Already he spent little time there, most of his days being occupied at the smithy, Jacob having taught him much and professed that there was sufficient work for there to be a job with him, should he want it. It only remained to find suitable accommodation situated close by before he would be on his way. There was no doubt either that Nathaniel Hewitt would take the cloth. Jack would be happy to sponsor him when a position could be found. He was never without pain but his new-found faith had, it seemed, given him the means to deal with it.

True to her word, Becky had visited Pru a number of times at the dower house but had found her home only once. She had twice hunted down her quarry, for nothing was more certain than that she would find her niece at the rehabilitation centre. As it happened, Prudence was engaged with one of the men on the occasion of her first call, but Captain Staveley was standing in the yard and he greeted her.

"How delightful to see you, Mrs Jarvis. I trust you are well. And your husband."

"Thank you, yes. Benjamin is engaged in a business meeting in Wells today, so it seemed a good opportunity for me to see my niece. Is she here?"

"She is, but I believe she is at present involved in some aspect of remedial work with one of the soldiers and I think it would be inadvisable to interrupt. Perhaps you would like instead to come to the house where I can offer you some refreshment."

"I had far rather take a drive about the estate, if you would join me."

As he was aware that Becky was an accomplished whip, Jack was more than happy to concur. They drove for a while in companionable silence before she was moved to say, "Forgive me if I presume too much, but I would ask you a question."

"Ask away," he replied, wondering what might be coming next from this unconventional woman.

"I have known you for a little while now, Captain, and though we met infrequently I am fairly certain that I have your measure. Prudence I have known for less time but in much closer proximity." Jack stiffened but made no reply and Becky continued. "I am aware, for you have both confided in me, that you used to be close friends in the past. Of late, though, it seems to me that there has been a cooling between you. Have you had a falling out? Is there anything I might do to bring you back together?"

It was not to be expected that Jack would lay bare his feelings. A man who had long ago learned to keep his own counsel, he had himself well in control. There was no way Becky would cajole any information from him. "You mistake," he said, affably enough. "We are working together each day. I think it unlikely we would be able to do so under the circumstances you describe."

"I trust I have not offended you. I am fond of you both, but shall say no more on this head. Be assured, however, that I would be happy to intervene in the future, should you so wish."

"My dear Mrs Jarvis, there is nothing amiss, I assure you."

She allowed it to pass but she was not for one moment fooled. An observer of people, she was easily able to see beyond the façade Jack had erected. The man was hurting, no doubt about it. Becky had not as yet confronted Prudence, deeming that she would receive short shrift were she to broach the subject. But something needed to be done to bring these two together, for nothing was more certain than that they should make a match of it. She sighed inwardly and turned the subject but determined to find some solution, for both were stubborn and it would take much to break down the barrier that now existed between them.

"I understand that you have significant plans for expansion. I must tell you, sir, that I am filled with admiration for the work you are doing here."

The awkward moment passed and Jack spoke with enthusiasm about his hopes for the future. He confided in her that finding occupation for the men in the time after they completed their recovery programme was a problem he would have to bend his mind to.

"I would be happy to give a position to some, if appropriate, and I know I speak for my husband when I say he would feel the same. There is always work to be done on a property the size of Honeysuckle Cottage, either on the building itself or the land surrounding it. Am I right in thinking that the men would be best suited to some kind of physical activity, accustomed as they are to being outdoors and toiling in all weathers?"

"I can only say that from my own experience I become far less than affable if I find no outlet for my physical energy. These men are, I am certain, the same. You may be sure I shall approach you." He smiled warmly at her. "I only hope you do not come to regret your offer, for over time there will be many who will require such assistance as you have tendered. I thank you most sincerely."

"Nonsense," she said, but she was happy once again to be on terms with him.

CHAPTER TWENTY-TWO

The puppies had proved to be a great hit. Dafydd Morgan remained at the centre only two more weeks and, with Jacob's approval, took one of them with him. A small cottage was made available to him and his aptitude with the crutches matched that of his newly acquired skill at the smithy. He had reached a level of independence far beyond what might have been hoped for when first he had arrived at Fairham, and he had become optimistic for the future because he felt useful once more.

Jack had charged Simpkins with the task of finding a suitable position for Nathaniel Hewitt, and all that remained now was for the details to be finalised. He was to become the incumbent of a small parish situated some considerable distance away, but none involved in his welfare had any doubt as to his prospects for success or the need to return. Hewitt had become a man reborn and would carve a future for himself and be an example to those he had pledged to serve. Willingly would Captain Staveley be his sponsor. He only wished it might be as easy to resolve the problems of those who remained.

And then an unforeseen disaster struck. Skerrit had somehow escaped the confines of his room without escort and, for reasons that no-one could understand, had strangled one of the puppies. Prudence was heartbroken and against all advice confronted him. Jack, following hard upon her heels, arrived in time to see the soldier draw and raise a knife with the obvious intention of using it upon the furious woman who had presumed to challenge him. Throwing himself between them,

Jack took the blow that was meant for her. He fell to the ground, blood pouring from a wound in his chest where the weapon was still lodged. Prudence sank to her knees beside him, white as a sheet, while others rushed to restrain Skerrit.

"Someone fetch Doctor Ellis," she said in a voice far removed from her normal tones. "And a stretcher. We cannot leave him here on the floor. We must carry him to a bed. Fitz, help me here. Oliver, the doctor!" Her voice grew louder and more urgent.

Oliver Hervey rushed off to do her bidding and Fitz engaged the help of another while Pru kept pressure on the wound in an effort to staunch the flow. Unsure whether or not to remove the blade, she let it remain where it was. It could do no more damage than it already had, and she had no wish to promote further bleeding. Skerrit was man-handled away and locked in his room, there being no lack of volunteers to guard the door. Bunting appeared, having heard the commotion, and he fetched a stretcher and helped Fitz to carry Jack to one of the beds.

"John, I would move him to the house. To his own room, where he will be more comfortable," Pru said.

"I must advise against such action. Forgive me, but I have more experience than you in such circumstances. The less we move him the better. Wiser to wait and see what the doctor has to say. I dare say Lieutenant Hervey will bring him here with all haste."

"But what can we do?" Pru cried, a note of panic creeping into her voice.

"There is naught we can do, other than keep pressure on that wound, which you are doing already. Perhaps it might be best if you let me take over and you organise hot water and towels in readiness for the doctor's arrival."

Grateful for something to do, Pru sped off on trembling limbs to follow his instructions. She was in no doubt as to the severity of the wound. Jack would be lucky to see this day out. Had she distrusted her own instincts she had only to look at the silent tears streaming down the batman's face. She found herself silently praying.

It was some time before Doctor Ellis arrived, Hervey having tracked him down at the home of another patient and practically dragged him away. By the time they reached the centre at Fairham, Jack had lost a considerable amount of blood and the doctor remarked that it was only thanks to their quick action in staunching the flow that he was still alive. All were dismissed save for John Bunting, whose services were required.

"It's obvious you have some idea of what you're doing. Learned a lot in the field, did you?"

"You might say that." He looked Doctor Ellis directly in the eye. "I've been with Captain Staveley for a number of years now. Many's the time he's been in mortal danger, but I never thought to see him die at home at the hands of someone he was trying to help."

Doctor Ellis returned his gaze unwaveringly. "I won't try to fool you. It's a grave situation, but don't despair. We haven't lost him yet. Been unconscious all the time, has he?"

"In and out, you might say. Seemed to be struggling to mention something, but since he did we haven't had a peep out of him."

"And what might that have been, if you don't mind me asking? Was it decipherable?"

Bunting remembered how Jack had clutched at his arm while he was leaning over his chest. "Quiet, it was, but clear as what you're saying to me now. Seems he thought Miss Fairham might feel she was to blame for what happened. 'Not her fault,' he said to me. 'Tell her, John, it wasn't her fault.' That was all, but he felt easier, I think. Then he relapsed into unconsciousness again and has remained so."

Doctor Ellis thought that was just as well and said as much. What he was about to do would be painful enough. He cut Jack's clothes away to cause the least agitation, for there was no way shirt and coat could be removed in the normal way. While doing so, he instructed Bunting to take one of the pieces of cloth Prudence had brought in and to fold it four times over to form a pad. Then he withdrew the knife, telling Bunting to press the pad immediately to the wound and to hold it firm while he applied bandages to hold it in place.

"It's a deep cut, but I am satisfied it has not penetrated any vital organs. Between you and me, he'd have been a goner by now if that had been the case. Right," he said, standing again, "there's little we can do now other than wait."

"Miss Fairham wanted to move him to his own bedchamber at the manor. We judged it to be too dangerous, but perhaps now, with him being bound up and all?"

"Well, I wouldn't like to see him manhandled too much. Certainly it will do him no good to be jostled about in a carriage, but if you think you can carry him on a stretcher then yes, I agree he would be better off there."

John gave him to understand that there would be no shortage of volunteers to carry Jack back to the manor, and Doctor Ellis said he would remain at Fairham until the captain was settled in his own bed. They opened the door to find Prudence sitting quietly on a chair immediately outside, her hands wringing a crumpled kerchief. Fitz and Hervey were with her, having sent everyone else about their business, and it was they who took charge of the patient with that special gentleness that large men sometimes display. Bunting went ahead to make things ready at the house and Prudence and Doctor Ellis followed behind. As they neared the house she stumbled and, but for his hand at her elbow, would have fallen.

"Thank you, Doctor Ellis. Forgive me, you have far more important things to worry about than a hysterical woman. You must find it hard to believe I am a soldier's daughter."

"On the contrary, Miss Fairham, I think you have conducted yourself with great dignity and restraint. It is my understanding from something that Mr Bunting tells me that you might feel in some way to blame for this sad affair."

"It is most certainly my fault. Had I not reacted in the way I did, Captain Staveley would not now be lying on a stretcher in danger of losing his life. I behaved like a distraught child. Indeed, I was distraught, but that is no excuse for my actions. Are you aware of what happened?"

"Not the details, no."

She stopped, and he with her. She turned to speak to him and he was able to see the anguish writ clearly on her features. "You warned me before to stay clear of Skerrit, did you not? If only I had taken heed, but the circumstances were such that … well, I must tell you that for reasons I am unable to fathom he strangled one of the puppies we have here. Like a fool I confronted him. The blow that Jack took was meant for me, Doctor. He saw it coming and flung himself between us."

"So naturally you blame yourself. If anyone is to blame it is Skerrit, though the poor fellow is out of his mind. I am of the opinion that you can do no more for him here and that he must be assigned to an asylum. Is it my fault, do you think, that I did not see this coming, or something like it? We are all the victims of circumstance, Miss Fairham. No more than you do I consider myself to be culpable. Sometimes our judgement is perhaps not as good as we might wish, but I don't think anyone could have foreseen this happening."

Jack had by now been carried up the steps into the house and they turned again to follow. It seemed to Doctor Ellis that his patient well knew what the lady's reaction would be. So much so that he had striven to exonerate her, with what he must have known might be his last words. Doctor Ellis repeated to Pru what Bunting had told him. "So you see, this is one of those unhappy situations when something untoward has happened, but it does not follow that anyone is to blame."

"You are a kind man, Doctor, and I know you mean well, but there is no doubt in my mind where the blame lies. If Jack dies, I must carry this with me for the rest of my life."

An hour later, having seen Jack safely to his chamber, Doctor Ellis took his leave. "I shall return tomorrow to check on my patient and, if required, to change the dressing. If you have any anxiety in the meantime, I will come if called. Would you like me to escort you to the dower house on my way home, Miss Fairham?"

"That is kind of you, Doctor Ellis, but I have the intention of remaining here until we know how things stand. I have already asked Mrs Jenkins to prepare my old bedchamber, but between us John Bunting and I will keep watch over Jack. He or I will remain with him at all times."

"Then I shall see you in the morning." Doctor Ellis paused before adding, "It is possible the captain's condition will appear to worsen during the night. I have given him what medication I can to keep him calm, but there is every chance he will become restless. I leave it to you to judge whether or not to send for me."

"I shall try not to do so, Doctor. I pray it will not be necessary."

It had taken some considerable time to settle Jack, the doctor wishing to reassure himself that moving his patient had caused no renewed bleeding. The rest of his clothes had been removed with Bunting's aid, an ordeal which though he was unconscious quite evidently took its toll, for he mumbled and moaned a few times while it was being done. During the time all this was taking place, Prudence had taken charge of the house once more. She suggested that Fitz and Hervey return home overnight as there was little they could do, but there was no moving them.

"And who do you think will ride to fetch the doctor, should it become necessary? Bunting will not leave Jack's side, I know. If it is not putting Mrs Jenkins to too much trouble, we would spend the night at Fairham, eh, Fitz?"

"Well, I for one have no intention of going anywhere tonight."

"Then I shall ask the cook to provide supper for us all, though I do not at present feel any desire to eat," Pru replied, grateful to have their support.

"Nor I," said Oliver, "but we will be of little use to Jack if we are weak with hunger."

"I shall relieve Bunting for an hour or so until then and will join you later in the dining room, gentlemen."

Prudence entered Jack's room. It seemed eerily quiet and Bunting was standing motionless by his master's bed. It was a room she knew well, for it had been her father's and there had been times as a child when she had been permitted to visit him in his chamber, though she had not been there in recent years. While Angus may have had to endure the hardships of war while abroad, he had ensured that when home no comfort was denied him. The room had an air of opulence about it that was at odds with the major's financial status, but it had been furnished at a time when he had been in funds from an unexpectedly large win at the card table. Pru had little regard for her surroundings, however, as she stepped resolutely towards the large four-poster. Bunting moved aside to make room for her but she followed him to the window.

"Fitz and Olly are to stay overnight, John," she said in hushed tones. "Go now and eat, and I will stay until your return. Before you come back, perhaps you could ask Mrs Jenkins for a truckle bed to be set up at the side of this room. It is my intention that either you or I will remain here at all times."

"Surely you will not sleep in this room, Miss Prudence!" Bunting said, more than a little shocked. She dismissed his uneasiness impatiently.

"What, do you think I care for convention when Jack may be dying and I the cause? Put aside this foolishness. It does not become you."

Bunting subsided and, truth to tell, he would be glad of her aid. He had spent his whole life at the manor or on the battlefield in the service of Major Fairham and subsequently Captain Staveley. With no kin of his own, they and Pru had become his family. He needed no further persuasion and left to do her bidding. Alone now with Jack, she moved back to the bed and sank onto the chair that was placed beside it. He looked unnaturally pale, almost white against the sheets, and had been positioned to lie on his back with his arms at his sides. The thought crossed her mind that thus would lie a corpse and, able now to give vent to her emotions which she had so well kept in check in front of others, she wept long and silently. Finally, with no more tears to shed, she took his hand in hers. It felt dry and somehow parched. She raised it against her cheek.

"What have I done, Jack? You have been my hero these many years. When first my father brought you home and I saw you in your uniform, well, let me only say that it is unfair to introduce a girl to a man wearing his regimentals," she said, smiling briefly at the memory. "But I regarded you as a big brother. At least that's what I have told myself for so long. How blind are we who choose not to see!" He remained as still and silent as ever, the only sign of life the shallow movement of his chest as he breathed. Secure in the knowledge that he could not hear her, she poured out her heart to him. "I realise now that I have loved you forever and I promise, if only you will get better, that we will put aside this foolish disagreement that has lain between us like an insurmountable boulder. I know you can never regard me as anything but a sister. I understand that. But if we may only be friends again, I would ask no more." Her voice broke as finally she said, "Don't leave me, Jack," and once more the tears began to flow.

When Bunting returned a while later, there was no sign of her previous perturbation. She had used the time well. For a start she had opened the window a little way to allow the air to circulate in the room, then opened the door to a gentle knock when a footman brought the bed. This was set by the wall furthest away from the patient and a screen was moved to shield it from his sight — if only he would wake up — and from the morning sunlight that would come flooding into the room. Mrs Jenkins came herself to make up the bed, for she knew that Miss Fairham would be sorely distressed.

"If there's anything I can do for the captain you only have to ask, miss. Such a kind gentleman he is, and it grieves me to see him so."

Though the other woman's obvious anxiety served to show what loyalty Jack had engendered in his staff, it did nothing to aid Prudence, who was struggling with her own emotions. Asking only that she assemble lavender and pine cones in a bowl and return with them as soon as possible, she managed to usher the faithful woman out of the room. When John Bunting came in shortly afterwards, he found the atmosphere much fresher. The potpourri exuded a reassuring fragrance and a candle was set in readiness on a small table by the bed, the better to observe their patient later when it became dark. In addition, either he or Prudence might be able to read during their vigil. "I shall make some lemonade and bring it with me when I come back."

Bunting looked questioningly at her and she smiled weakly.

"You will think me mad, I know, but even if he does not wake we might moisten his lips. It will perhaps be refreshing. Now, I must join the others and at least pretend that I have some appetite. I will return in a few hours to relieve you, at which time I hope you will retire to your own chamber, John, for we both must keep up our strength. When the time comes, I shall lay down on the bed here and you may come in the morning to see how he goes on."

Bunting was reluctant to agree to this arrangement and said so, but she insisted that sleep was important to them both, for the care of their patient would be long and wearisome. She left him to sit with Jack and went for her supper.

"And if he dies, what then will happen to the centre?" were the words Prudence heard as she entered the dining room.

"You shall not speak so, Fitz," she said quietly. "What, would you bury the man while he lies still breathing above stairs?"

Fitz was mortified, but Oliver took up cudgels in his defence. They had been discussing Skerrit, he said, and knew of the doctor's advice that he be sent to an asylum for the insane. Even if Jack were to survive, there were men in their care and others on the way whose futures could not be set aside just because their benefactor was incapacitated or worse.

"Just!" Pru exclaimed, the word bursting from her lips. Oliver chose to ignore it.

"We have decided that Fitz and I should escort Skerrit, if not tomorrow then certainly the next day, to a place where he and others with whom he would come into contact might be safe from harm. He will have to be bound, of course, but we can see no other way. We wait only for Ellis's recommendation. We are all of us conscious that none of this is the poor man's fault and can only grieve for him, but the safety of the rest is of paramount importance."

"I agree he must go," said Pru. "Naturally we cannot succeed in every case, but to declare I am saddened that our first failure must end this way is, to say the very least, a gross understatement. I have tried these past few hours to blame him for what occurred, but that would be unjust and untrue. Mine is the blame for acting so foolishly."

It was Fitz who spoke next, filling their glasses. "No-one is to blame but the damned war that changed forever the lives of so many good men. I suggest, Miss Fairham, that you look now to the future. What is past cannot be changed and we must do what we can to mend those who have been broken. We leave Jack's care to you and Bunting. You must trust us for the time being to continue the work at the centre. I hope we will not be away above two days, but there are staff enough now to continue without us for a short time. Meanwhile, I suggest you eat something, not only to maintain your strength but also not to give offence to Cook who has tried so hard to tempt us all." He stood for a moment and raised his glass. "I am more proud than I can say to have served with the major and the captain. Without men like them, this world would be a harder place. I drink to the memory of one and to the recovery of the other."

When Prudence went to Jack's bedchamber a while later, she found Bunting standing by the bed as before. He was as still as the man who lay before him, and in the flickering light of the candle she could see the anguish that engulfed him. It took all Pru's entreaties to persuade him to go and get some rest.

"And will you get some sleep?" he demanded gruffly.

"It is my intention to remain awake, and I have brought with me a book to bear me company. If needs be, I will lay down upon the truckle bed over there and close my eyes. I will return to my own chamber in the morning, when I hope to get some sleep while I leave the captain in your care."

Both knew it to be a fallacy that she might close her eyes when there was no-one else present to watch over Jack, but Bunting knew it was futile to argue and left the room. Pru did not immediately open her book but sat beside the bed, once more holding Jack's hand, reasserting her feelings. It seemed, now that she had recognised the true nature of her emotions, she had a need to share them with this man she so loved.

She could perceive no change in him to begin with but, after a while, his cheeks became flushed and his body moved fitfully, seemingly of its own volition. She placed a wet cloth upon his forehead but, delirious now, he threw his head from side to side and she withdrew. During one of his quieter moments, Pru attempted to wet his lips with the lemonade she had prepared but as the night went on it became obvious, even to her inexperienced eyes, that Jack was getting worse. He began moaning and muttering and, where before she had wished only that he would not lie so still and lifeless, she now would have given much for him to recapture that peace. Fearful that the convulsive movements would cause the bleeding to start again, she pulled down the covers to examine the dressing. It remained intact with no sign of seepage, and she blessed Doctor Ellis for his good work. She was more than once tempted to send for him but recalled that he had said Jack would likely get worse during the small hours. As the sky began to lighten, there was a tap on the door and Bunting entered.

"I could wait no longer, Miss Prudence. How does he fare?"

"He has not had a good night, John, and has been in a fever for much of the time. If you will stay with him, I will go and lie on my own bed for an hour or two until the doctor arrives. See if you can moisten his lips with the lemonade. It seemed to give him some small amount of relief when I did so. I would beg that you call for me if there is any further change."

She left the room and almost fell over the chair that had been placed in the corridor. It appeared that the faithful batman had not after all retired but had sat guard all night outside the door. She smiled briefly. If the love of his companions could help Jack pull through, they might all be assured of his recovery.

CHAPTER TWENTY-THREE

Prudence had lain on her bed fully clothed in anticipation of the doctor's visit and a tap on the door brought her immediately awake two hours later. She sped to Jack's room to find Doctor Ellis had completed his examination.

"It is as I thought. Bunting has advised me that Captain Staveley passed a restless night and that the fever is upon him. I should have been extremely surprised had that not been the case and thank you for your common sense in not calling me out, for it must now run its course and there is little we can do but wait."

A twisted smile flashed across Pru's features and she said, "You may be sure I was many times tempted to do so. Are you happy with how he goes on?"

"Happy? Not the word I would have used. I do not want to raise your expectations, Miss Fairham. The captain is by no means yet out of danger, but he is a soldier and a fighter. If anyone can overcome such a wound, it is he. Now, if you'll excuse me, Lieutenants Fitzroy and Hervey met me on arrival and gave me to understand they wish to speak to me before I leave. I shall return again tomorrow morning. In the meantime, you and Bunting are doing all that is required. He needs your combined strength, and I know I can rely on you."

With that he left the room and Pru and Bunting regarded each other wordlessly before he too excused himself. She sat once more by the bed and laid the back of her hand on Jack's forehead, but he thrust it away and the tears which seemed to come so readily fell once more.

"You wished to see me, gentlemen?" Doctor Ellis said, encountering the friends in the hall. They invited him to join them in the library.

"We will not keep you long, Doctor, but there are two things we would ask of you," Oliver said when they were all seated. "Our most pressing concern is for Captain Staveley. Neither of us has seen him since we brought him back to the house yesterday, and we are not inclined to press Miss Fairham or Bunting too much on his progress." He looked from the doctor to Fitz and back again. "Is there progress? We have seen too many die in the field to be sanguine about his chances and would ask that you be open with us."

There was little he could tell them, he asserted, other than that Jack was now in the full throes of a perilous fever. "Frankly it could go either way, but I would not say as much to Miss Fairham. I am happy to leave him in her care. She is sensible, and as a soldier's daughter I am confident she will rise to any challenge. There is little we can do now but wait. You said there were two things?"

It was Fitz who this time expressed their concerns. "We are keen to do what we can to resolve the situation regarding Skerrit, and as speedily as possible. I fear his mind is irreparably damaged, poor man, and that there is nothing more we can do for him here. I understand you are of the opinion that he would be better placed in an asylum and we look to you to advise us."

Ellis agreed that was the case and gave them an address not one day's full ride from Fairham. He wrote a note to the principal outlining what had occurred and asked that any expenses be directed to Captain Jack Staveley at Fairham Manor.

"You must have some confidence, then, in his survival," Hervey said.

"I always prefer to err on the side of optimism. I find it helps me as well as my patients. If there is nothing else, please excuse me. I must get on. As I have already told Miss Fairham, I shall return tomorrow but in all probability you will not yourselves be back yet. Good morning, gentlemen."

He left and Fitz and Hervey set about making arrangements for the transfer of Skerrit and the return to a normal schedule for the remaining residents.

When Bunting relieved Pru some two hours later she almost ran to her room, aware that she was still wearing the clothes she had put on yesterday. A glance in the mirror showed wisps of hair sticking out in all directions and she wondered what the doctor must have thought of her. She rang immediately for Kitty, who aided her out of her dress and went to fetch some water so that she might wash. In less time than might have been imagined she was once more her neat self and she went in search of Fitz and Olly, only to find they had already departed.

Exhausted but in need of something to do, for Bunting would not yet relinquish his place, she knew, Prudence went to the centre to check that all was well. It was no secret that Jack had been wounded, perhaps mortally, and every man in turn expressed their concern. Whatever loyalty these soldiers might have shown their commanding officer during their service had now been transferred to Captain Staveley and there wasn't one among them who would not have given his own life for him. There was little she could tell them but she tried hard to be reassuring while at the same time not raising any false hopes. She went to see Dash, who was ecstatic at the sight of her and ran around in circles. Prudence smiled with genuine pleasure for the first time in two days. "Yes, and I am delighted to see you too, but this is not acceptable behaviour," she said, kneeling down and tickling the puppy's tummy. On impulse she had Firefly saddled up and, though not dressed for riding, went for a canter and returned considerably more refreshed than an hour's sleep might have left her.

Back in Jack's room and feeling much invigorated, she sat and read aloud, hoping the sound of her voice, of any voice, would act in some way as a stimulation. She had set another small table beside her on which stood the lemonade, a small bowl of water and a flannel and from time to time she set down the book to wipe Jack's brow or wet his lips. She could not flatter herself that it helped, for his jerky movements continued. However, when she rose to leave, she took his hand and it seemed there was a slight pressure on her own. More hopeful than she had been for many long hours, she exchanged a few words with Bunting. "I wondered if it might not be a good idea to talk to Jack about your campaigns, perhaps giving him something to focus on in his delirium. I feel sure I couldn't have imagined it. I am convinced he was trying to communicate with me." There was a slight relaxation in Bunting's tight shoulders and Pru realised that it would be a relief for him also to have something to do.

After that, having partaken of a light meal, Pru went to bed and slept for many hours. She awoke with a guilty start, for it was now dark outside and Bunting would have been at his post far beyond what was intended. Hurrying to relieve him, she entered the room to a strange silence. It took her a moment to appreciate that Jack was no longer thrashing about and that the batman was sitting on the chair next to his bed, head buried in his hands. She started forward, all hope now abandoned, but at her approach Bunting looked up and he was smiling.

"The fever's broken, Miss Pru! Only moments ago. He's done it! He's going to be all right! I was about to send for you but, well, I…" She could see that this big man with a huge heart had once more been crying, only this time they were tears of joy. "I'll leave you now and send a message to the doctor. Just to let him know, though we shall see him here in the morning."

"Thank you, John. For everything."

Pru sat once more by Jack, moving the candle the better to see his face. Gone was the flushed demeanour. Gone too the involuntary thrashing about of his limbs. He lay calmly, not awake but not entirely asleep either. This time, when she took his hand in hers, there was no doubt. Pressure was returned by pressure. Jack was back.

CHAPTER TWENTY-FOUR

By the time Doctor Ellis called the next morning, Jack was sitting up in bed and paying attention. Though still very weak and in considerable pain, a fact which he did not impart to his nurses, his entire demeanour had changed and there was about him a devilish spirit. Every so often a smile of pure mischief played upon his lips. For Jack had a secret. It was one he did not wish to share at the present time, feeling himself too debilitated to act upon it, but it was enough just to enjoy it for the while. Not only was he alive but he had been given hope! Not all of Pru's outpourings had fallen upon deaf ears. Some had penetrated his delirium; had given him the will to live.

"Good morning, Doctor. Please forgive me for not rising to greet you. I must thank you for your services, for I have no doubt I would be a dead man were it not for you."

"Thanks are unnecessary, Captain Staveley. I am happy to see you in such good spirits and have no doubt you will now make a recovery, if you obey my instructions," he said sardonically. "I have met many of your sort before, and I make no doubt you would leave your bed now if you were able to stand. Am I not right?"

Jack had the grace to look sheepish.

"You will remain where you are and I shall return tomorrow when I will once more change your bandages. You will be bedridden for at least another two or three days. Then, and only then, might I permit you to be carried downstairs for an hour or two." He raised an eyebrow as if expecting Jack to argue with him but perceived only an expression of meek acceptance. "I expect Lieutenants Fitzroy and Hervey will by then have returned. Between them and the good Bunting they should be able to manage it without doing you any harm."

"They are away?"

"Yes. It was considered by all, in the light of what has happened, that Fairham is not a suitable place for Skerrit. Sadly he had gone beyond the point where you could help him. They have at my instruction taken the poor chap to an asylum for the insane. It is a place I know and I am confident he will be treated well and no longer be in a position to harm anyone else."

A look of pain that had nothing to do with his injury passed across Jack's face.

"Do not distress yourself, Captain Staveley. To put it in familiar terms, you are fighting a war. You cannot win every battle."

Doctor Ellis left soon after and Prudence and Bunting came back into the room. Pru was all bustling efficiency as she moved the screen a little and adjusted the pillows. She had expected an argument, but Jack submitted with a mildness that was surprising for one who did not like fuss. She put it down to the fact that he was still very weak, but she was happy that he seemed not to be treating her with the coolness he had shown before the attack. Lifting the jug from the small bedside table, she said she would return with some fresh lemonade.

"And will you then sit and read to me for a while?" Jack asked, smiling serenely.

"Of course. If that is what you wish."

"I should like nothing more."

She was finding it very difficult to deal with him in this strange mood. It was enough to keep her own feelings under control, for nothing was more certain than that she must strive to maintain some kind of balance. She resolved never again to

215

return to that awful time when they were so at odds with each other.

Fitz and Olly returned in the middle of the afternoon and Prudence left them to entertain Jack for a while. Doctor Ellis returned the next morning as promised and changed the dressings, assuring his patient that things were healing nicely but ordering that he remain two more days in his room. "You have my permission to go downstairs thereafter, and with that you must be content. I too am in the habit of command and I expect to have my orders obeyed." Jack did not miss the smile in the doctor's eyes and, though disappointed, promised to acquiesce.

His convalescence was steady, aided — once he was permitted to go downstairs — by the many visits he received from friends and neighbours, for he would else have gone mad. Those who came to see him would find him on the terrace, the weather being kind. On occasion he would play cards, though he resorted to doing so only indoors after a sudden gust of wind blew them from the table. Sometimes he could be found reading a book, but he was essentially a man of action and found it difficult to concentrate. He was impatient too for another reason. That Prudence cared for him as much as he for her he now knew to be true but, much as he longed to declare himself and crush her in his arms, he could not do so in his present state. Determined to instil his proposal with all the romance his heart's desire could wish, he bided his time.

Mr and Mrs Jarvis were perhaps his most frequent visitors and, as they drove over once more to see him, Becky asked her husband if he did not agree that Prudence and Jack were well suited and that something should be done to bring about an alliance between them.

"You will do no such thing, Rebecca," Benjamin said in a voice far sterner than the one he usually employed with his wife. "It is not for us to interfere."

"But Benjamin, my love, I would only have them as happy as we are ourselves."

"Impossible! No one could be."

She was delighted at his response and abandoned her cajoling to link her arm through his, for it was he who was driving. This did not, however, prevent her from turning the problem over in her mind, as she had done many times, trying to find a solution.

"I am heartened to see you have made so much progress since last we visited," Becky said soon after they arrived.

"I should not dare it to be otherwise, for between Bunting and these three," Jack said, gesturing to include Prudence, Fitz and Olly, "I could not fail to have improved."

Squeezing her husband's hand under the table in apology, for she did not like to go against his deliberately stated wishes, Becky continued without any change of expression, "It will be time soon, I expect, to make arrangements for the wedding."

Pru was taken aback and looked at her aunt with startled eyes. "What can you be saying? There is no talk of marriage. What, I…" She lowered her eyes again, confused and greatly distressed.

"Come, my child. Any fool can see that the pair of you are besotted with each other. Do you tell me, Jack, that you have not yet proposed to my niece?"

Jack was well aware that he needed to tread carefully. "Becky, you know I adore you, but I should be grateful if you would leave me to make my own declaration," he said, turning to the lady in question.

Pru raised her gaze to meet his. "I see how it is. You think you have compromised me because I have stayed here without a chaperon. We are friends. That is all. You cannot love me."

He took her hand in his. "I do not believe I have compromised you, and much you care for such fustian anyway. I hope we will always be friends but no, that is not all. I love you with all my heart and will do whatever it takes to win you, Pru. Your aunt, and — judging by their silence — Fitz and Olly too, and no doubt Benjamin, are all well aware of my feelings for you. I was waiting only until I was as sound of body as I am of mind to tell you that my life would be meaningless without you. Since it is the obvious expectation of our acquaintance, please do not refuse me. I would hate to disappoint them."

Pru's look was unwavering. A small sigh escaped her lips and a smile reached from deep in her heart to her now shining sapphire eyes. She placed her other hand in his. "Then we must not do so, must we?"

Fitz, who was sitting next to him, slapped Jack on the shoulder, causing him to clutch at his wound. "Get off me, you brute. I am a sick man," he exclaimed, but he was laughing.

Hands were wrung. Hugs were exchanged. In view of the outcome, Becky was forgiven by her husband and, after embracing her much-loved niece, she said, "I wish you as happy as I am myself. I could ask no more for you." Turning to the others, she added, "I think we should all now leave these two to discuss their future."

Left alone, Pru and Jack sat in happy silence for a few minutes before he stood and drew her to her feet. "You cannot know, my love, how desolate I have been. It was only your voice, calling to me as if from some great distance, that brought me back from the brink."

"You heard?"

"I heard." He lifted her chin with one finger and laid his lips upon hers, and she melted into his arms. Some minutes later, seated once again, he said, "I think Angus would have approved, do you not, Pru?"

"Without a doubt. My only sadness is that he will not be here to give me away when we are joined as man and wife. I shall entreat my Uncle William instead to perform that service for me."

Pru and Jack waited only for the banns to be read and were married with almost unseemly haste. They did not care. In the meantime, Prudence had removed once more to the dower house at Jack's insistence. She knew not why he was so adamant but acquiesced readily enough, for soon she would have her heart's desire. "After all the work that has been done there, it is a shame for it to go to waste," he said. They discussed the possibility of Fitz and Olly moving there to be on hand for their future work. "It must be tedious for them to travel there and back each day. Particularly now that we are expanding. Tell me, my darling, where would you like to go for your honeymoon?" She looked at him, serene, content and knowing that at last happiness was hers. "If you would be in agreement, Jack, I should like to remain here."

And so it was. As they returned from the church to Fairham for their wedding breakfast, Jack took her hand and led her over the threshold. Only then did she ask, "Why, Jack, were you so insistent that I return to the dower house after we were betrothed?"

"Can you not understand, my love? I have waited many months to say this, and I think these words must never before have had greater meaning. Prudence, with all my heart I say welcome home."

A NOTE TO THE READER

Dear Reader

As I type this early in September it is at the end of a disappointing summer, weather-wise. However, as often happens, the season is not quite ready to leave us yet and a late burst is promised for the coming week. Bed linen is blowing gently on the line in the early morning sunshine and I've promised myself some reading time this afternoon in my favourite garden chair.

I hope you've enjoyed *When Only Pride Remains*. I think there are many of us who allow our pride to stand in the way. On the whole I see it as a strength and certainly I believe it helped Prudence when tragedy struck. I also believe there is time to let it go.

If you would consider leaving a review on **Amazon** or **Goodreads**, it would be much appreciated, though I would be just as happy if you'd like to join me on my **Facebook author page** for a chat. You can also visit me on **Twitter**, **Instagram** and my **website**.

Thank you for reading and following.

Be well and I hope to see you next time.

Natalie

nataliekleinman.com

Sapere Books is an exciting new publisher of brilliant fiction and popular history.

To find out more about our latest releases and our monthly bargain books visit our website: **saperebooks.com**